Impound

GARY LEE VINCENT

Burning Bulb
PUBLISHING

Impound
By **Gary Lee Vincent**

Burning Bulb Publishing
P.O. Box 4721
Bridgeport, WV 26330-4721
United States of America
www.BurningBulbPublishing.com

Cover designed by Gary Lee Vincent with photographic elements from Gary Lee Vincent, Celeste Marcus (wolf-rabbit woman) and Pexel contributors Rachel Claire, Rene Asmussen, and Wilson Vitorino.

First Edition.

Paperback Edition ISBN: 978-1-948278-47-8

Printed in the United States of America

Also by Gary Lee Vincent

Novels
PASSAGEWAY
BELLY TIMBER
ATTACK OF THE MELONHEADS
WHEN THE BEDPOSTS SHAKE (RING OF THE SUCCUBUS)

Darkened—The West Virginia Vampire Series
DARKENED HILLS
DARKENED HOLLOWS
DARKENED WATERS
DARKENED SOULS
DARKENED MINDS
DARKENED DESTINIES

The Douglas River Vampire Series
RIVER: A VAMPIRE'S NIGHTMARE
ICARUS

Nonfiction
THE WINNER, THE LOSER
AGELATIONS
CONFIGURATION MANAGEMENT

Musical Releases
100 PERCENT
PASSION, PLEASURE, & PAIN
SOMEWHERE DOWN THE ROAD

Dedicated to John A. Russo,
my mentor, colleague, and friend.

PROLOGUE

15 Years Ago

It was night, close to midnight, and a cool wind was blowing through the West Virginian countryside. The forest was alive with animal and insect noises, rustles and squeaks and chirps of the native wildlife, as God's creatures attended to their nightly business.

In the midst of the forest, a short distance off of county route 44, was located an impound yard.

The trees pressed in on the chain-link fence that surrounded the vehicle yard, stopping just short of the wall of diamond-patterned wire mesh and leaving a border of grass around the perimeter.

To an observer outside of the mesh-ringed enclosure, at first glance the place would seem deserted; empty of human presence that was, with its sole occupants being the hundreds of cars arranged in doubled-up rows all the way across to the yard's opposite end.

However, all of the cars weren't all in one piece. Some of the vehicles were stripped down husks, and, as if the yard doubled as a scrapyard, strategically grouped parts of automobiles lay in neat stacks at points in it, oddly shaped chunks of metal and plastic that shone dully in the lambent moonlight. A faint smell of spilled automobile oil hung around those areas.

So yes, to anyone standing outside of the perimeter fence and looking in, the yard would at first appear to be empty of human life. And this, of course, would be a very reasonable assumption, considering this was the middle of the night, when most fine people were at home and in bed.

But a further glance would then reveal this not to be the case. One's eyes would quickly be drawn away from the rows of motor vehicles, down whichever pathway or driveway between the cars one stood nearest to, and instead focused over at a point in the middle of the yard, where fires seemed to be burning. And then one would quickly realize that one wasn't staring at just a single flame, but at a ring of them that was also suspended off the ground. One might almost think the distant ring of flame was a giant gas range.

But by then, he or she would have heard the accompanying chants; monotonous ritualistic sounds that grew loud and then soft, their tone and cadence seeming to ebb and flow with each gust of wind.

A ring of fires in midair at night in an impound yard? Chanting?

If that uneducated observer hadn't by then already fled, they would then conclude that something strange was happening out here for sure.

***

The ring of floating fires came from a circle of people—both male and female—standing in the middle of the array of cars, and who were holding up torches, the yard's electric security lights having all been temporarily switched off so that they could make use of the darkness to carry out their evil purpose.

With the lights off, it was hard to clearly make out the features of the torchbearers. However, one could tell that their garments were partly made of fur. The bodies of these men and women seemed to flicker as the flames danced.

The torchbearers were arranged around a strange altar on which lay a bound and gagged young man. Their captive had been stripped naked and his eyes stared wildly at his captors, his anxious gaze filled with questions; in his terror seeking both for some explanation as to what was happening to him, and for a way out of his predicament. He tugged desperately against his bonds, hoping to free himself. But the ropes were expertly tied and converted his exertions into futility.

The men and women continued chanting. Now their voices grew louder and louder still. Their faces, half-revealed by the flickering torchlight, were excited to the point of seeming crazed; with bulging eyes, slavering lips spread and twisted in manic grins, and bared teeth.

And still the noise of their chants increased, until soon it was unbearable to their captive—a manic crescendo of ritualistic insanity, inspiring nothing but the most intense terror; spine-chilling terror.

**

The next afternoon, a little girl skipped out the back door of her family's farmhouse into her backyard. The backyard was deserted at the moment; it was just her here and the trees and the grass. Over of the other side of the farmhouse she could hear the pigs. She could smell them too, when the reek from their pens blew over on the wind.

She paused once she was out there on the grass, sniffing in the sweet wholesome air, wrinkling up her cute little nose just like she did whenever mother baked brownies. It was a happy day, with sunshine falling on her through the branches of a tree whilst seeming to reflect off the corn crops out in the fields.

She felt like playing but her sister was asleep, and mother had said not to wake her up.

The little girl was six years old and impossibly cute in her yellow dress, polka dot blue smock, and her brunette pigtails. She stood still there in the backyard for a little while longer, watching the leaves of the tree ahead of her rustle in the wind. Then she lost interest in watching the leaves dance and took a few steps forward and stared up at the row of animal bones and teeth dangling like a mobile from one of the tree's lower branches and shifting with the wind.

The little girl giggled at the objects as they gently knocked against one another in the breeze. Then, as she usually did, she leaned up on tip-toes and tried to reach them. But even though adults could touch the bones and sometimes even complained that they'd been hung too low, she was too little to do so. She sighed, hoping she'd soon be taller.

Then she saw the bunny, hopping about on the grass a short distance away. She paused in delight and considered what to do.

"Hey, bunny wabbit!"

The rabbit froze where it was and turned towards her. With its pink nose twitching it, it regarded her cautiously, unsure if it should hop away from her or not. Then, seeing her pull out a carrot from the pockets of her smock and hold it out invitingly, the bunny hopped over towards her.

She knelt down and began feeding the rabbit the carrot. It ate hungrily, while she gently stroked it.

"Come on, baby bunny," she said after a while, picking up the rabbit and petting it, while it concentrated its attention on its unexpected meal. "Come on up to me!"

Still on her knees and with a smile on her face, she began singing to the rabbit. Her voice was babyish, but nonetheless sweet in its childish innocence:

"Rock-a-bye baby, in the treetop,

When the wind blows, the cradle will rock . . ."

And then suddenly, her angelic smile turned mean and her grip on the bunny tightened. The creature still instinctively ate its carrot, but it must have sensed danger to itself, because its small body tensed as her hold on it tightened, with her grip around its neck and forelegs becoming almost viselike.

"When the bough breaks, the cradle will fall . . ."

An evil gleam crossed the little girl's face. She twisted her hands in different directions and a sickening cracking sound echoed in the empty backyard.

She grinned down at the now lifeless bunny, its rear legs still kicking reflexively even though its life had departed. Once satisfied that it was dead, she scrambled back up to her feet and brushed the dirt from her bare knees.

Then, with the dead rabbit hanging limply from her hand and a thread of bloody saliva hanging limply from its mouth, the little girl skipped off around the side of the house, singing in that same sweet little-girl voice:

"And down will come baby, cradle and all . . ."

***

That night the little girl's father took her hunting. She'd gone hunting with him before, but this time was different because they were hunting a wolf. This was a big deal for the little girl. She clutched her hunting rifle with intense anticipation and had difficulty remaining quiet as she followed her father through the dark woods. Remaining quiet was hard for her anyway, as her pink Keystone Cricket bolt action .22 was almost as tall as herself and she couldn't help knocking it against things as she followed Father.

There was a wolf nearby, for sure. It was young, Father spotted it a few times on occasion near the pig pens and didn't much like it getting too close to the livestock. It was not much larger than a coyote, but still a wolf and, like a coyote, still a problem for the pigs, chickens, and cattle.

Father could sense the creature tonight and he was hoping his daughter wouldn't scare the beast away.

However, after Father had shushed her a couple times, he gave up on it and let the young girl enjoy the thrill of the chase.

The little girl liked nighttime, with its animal sounds, its creepy owl noises and the wind blowing through the trees.

Then, from a short distance ahead of them in the darkness, came the sound of a wolf howling.

"Shush," Father whispered to her. But his admonition was needless. She'd seen the pair of bright lupine eyes glittering in the darkness at the same time as he had and become as motionless as both he and the creature they were after.

The wolf had been eating a rabbit, but sensing the nearby human presence (maybe it had smelled them over the rabbit blood), it too had frozen in place.

"Okay, now, aim carefully at it," Father said. He was a tall and slim young man in his early twenties, handsome with dark eyes; and it was from him that his twin daughters had gotten their dark hair, not from his wife, who was a honey-blonde. While the little girl squatted in the brush and drew a careful bead on the wolf's head, Father also aimed the Redfield scope perched atop his higher powered Browning 30.06 at the wolf in case she missed, or maybe just wounded it.

But by either luck or good marksmanship, the little girl didn't miss. A rifle crack rang out in the night, and the wolf, which had seemed poised to flee its fate, hit the ground. The shot went clean through the wolf's left eye and hit true.

The recoil of the rifle made the girl lose her balance and hit the ground also.

"Did I get it, daddy? Did I? Did I kill the wolf?" she asked from her position flat on the grass.

"Well, let's just see now, girly!" Father said in amusement, leaning over to pull her up from the forest floor. "From where I'se currently standin', Mr. Wolf don't look to be going anywhere soon."

Together, hunting rifles in hand, they strode out of the undergrowth and examined the wolf. Father knelt beside the prone lupine body, examined it for a few seconds, and then wiped blood off his fingers onto the wolf's flanks.

"I reckon you did git it! Nice shot! Good girl!"

The little girl began jumping up and down excitedly, leaping and dancing around the wolf's carcass. "Can I flay it, daddy? I want to skin it. I'm a big girl now, daddy."

Father grinned up at her, his teeth bright in the moonlight. "Why, yes, you are, girly. You are indeed a big girl now. But best we let your sister flay it."

***

"And you will follow in Mommy's footsteps and bring in the spirits of the Wolf and the Rabbit. What do we know about the Rabbit?"

The question had been asked in a sing-song voice. The little girl fidgeted on her chair in the farmhouse living room and pondered the question. After a moment or two she grinned up at her mother, who, also smiling, was waiting patiently for her reply.

"The Rabbit is soft and fluffy," she replied.

Mother nodded. "Ye-es . . . and is it strong?"

She shook her little head and giggled. "Nooooo! It's weak! It's a varmint! I can kill it!"

Her mother nodded back at her. Mother was an attractive, well-proportioned woman, who nicely filled out her long brown dress, and the little girl wanted to grow up to be just like her. With an idle part of her mind, she wondered where her twin sister had gotten to; why she was the only one being quizzed here like this today. Usually, Mother taught them both. But then she remembered: Daddy had taken her sister with him to go visit Uncle Jim.

"Yes, the rabbit is weak and easily killed," Mother agreed, leaning over her young daughter, but what is good about it? What is good about the rabbit?"

The little girl instantly replied, "We can eat it! And it has fur! Wear its fur!"

Her mother, a visible intensity entering her eyes, nodded. "That's right. The Rabbit gives us food and keeps us alive. And it keeps us warm."

The little girl giggled and clapped her hands. "Yay!" Their recent lunch of rabbit stew was still warm in her tummy and she felt very alive, if a little bit drowsy, but she liked it when her mother instructed her like this about their family's ways. It was always exiting. And the afternoon sun shining in through the windows was reflecting off of Mother's hair and making it glow like gold and making Mother look oh so pretty.

"And what do we know about the Wolf?" Mother asked.

"It goes: 'Raaaar!' and 'Awooo-wooooh-woooooh!' "

"Yes . . . but what else, dearie? Do you remember what I said?"

She thought a little before replying, but not for long: "The wolf kills stuff! But . . . last night I killed it, didn't I, mamma? I killed the old wolf dead!"

Mother grinned broadly at her and pulled the voluminous skirt of her gown around her body. Now she had an almost feverish look on her face.

"That's right," she agreed. "You sure did kill the wolf dead yesternight. But remember, dearie, and don't you ever forget—the rabbit and the wolf are important to our people, because they are both part of nature."

The little girl clapped her hands and yelped excitedly. "And the clan likes nature, mamma. Huh?"

Mother nodded. "Yes, we do. The life cycle of nature. The rhythm of life, and death. And so, just like the wolf kills the rabbit—we can kill both the wolf and the rabbit. And we can kill more. The bigger the critter—the stronger, the smarter, the better. . . . We can use their life force. . . . Celebrate the goddess. And through each sacrifice, there is new life, reborn."

Her young daughter didn't really understand all this; she wasn't entirely sure what a 'life force' was. She was, after all, still in kindergarten. But one thing she did know for sure: and that was that celebrating the goddess was usually great fun, and Mother and Father had told she and her sister that there was gonna be a celebration tonight.

She couldn't wait.

***

It was nearly midnight again and, flaming torches in hand, the Clan were once more gathered around their strange altar, around their bound and naked captive.

They surrounded the altar and were in turn surrounded by the silent ranked multitude of vehicles, which were themselves surrounded by the enclosure's chain-link fence, with the forest encircling the entire lot.

The captive man stared at the throng from helpless and frantic eyes. After last night's ritual he'd been locked in a shed up at the north end of the yard. He had been fed during the day, given just sufficient food and water to keep him alive. He had pleaded for mercy but had instead been spat on and beaten up, the latter evidenced by the dark bruises that marred his otherwise pale complexion.

Now, with terror in his eyes and with his gag back in place, he once more struggled to break free from the ropes that secured him atop the crazy metal and bone construct his captors called their altar. His naked body glistened with sweat, and he struggled extra-hard as the torch-bearers closed in on the altar, their chanting seemingly growing louder with each step forward. Their chanting unnerved him.

And then, just when it seemed to the young man that his mind would break from sheer terror, the intensity of the chanting reduced.

The little girl's mother stepped forward. Her patchwork garment of rabbit skins marked her as the unmistakable leader of the occasion; the high priestess of whatever evil was being celebrated here. Her headdress had long furry rabbit ears.

She began speaking, and the chanting lowered in volume till it was merely a cascade of dark murmurs.

Once more, as when instructing her daughter in the afternoon, she spoke in a sing-song, as though entertaining children: "And just as the wolf preys on the rabbit, we prey on those weaker and less powerful than us."

While speaking, she stepped up close to the altar and ascended the two steps that brought her next to the captive. Over on the altar's farther side, her eyes locked first with those of her husband, who nodded approvingly back at her, and then she momentarily glanced down at her daughters, who stood one on either side of him, excitement written all over their young faces. Both of her little girls were grinning broadly.

The captive flinched as she brandished a knife at him, his eyes widening in even greater terror than before as she swept the long blade back and forth in the air above his torso, playing it across his throat and heart, his belly and genitals and back again. She swayed in a slow dance while doing this and kept speaking to her congregation, who now pressed in closer to the altar:

"We take their strength, and we take their spirit. With their life-force taken and added to our strength, our life-force grows more powerful."

While the captive shook his head and his eyes screamed "NO!" at her, she placed the knife on his neck and with one swift and expert slicing motion, slit his throat.

His eyes bulging in disbelief, the victim jerked as his blood spurted out into the night air, while the watchers groaned a collective sigh of pleasure.

"And with every new sacrifice," the priestess intoned, "with every drop of blood that is spilled, the clan grows in strength."

The dying man's blood splattered the altar table and collected into a gutter cut into the area directly beneath his neck. From here the blood ran into a large silvery goblet that had earlier been placed on a shelf attached to the altar. A wild-faced young man now stepped forward to monitor the collection of the blood.

The blood ran off the altar and filled the goblet. The young man removed the full goblet and replaced it with an empty one. He handed the full cup of blood to the priestess.

She accepted the full goblet from the young man and turned to face her congregation.

"And therefore," she said, "through the combined life force of prey and predator, of rabbit and wolf, we praise the goddess Oryctolupus."

After this proclamation, the priestess raised the goblet to her lips and drank from it. Then, her lips red with the shed blood, she handed the blood-filled goblet to the woman closest to her, who, after nodding at her, raised the goblet to her own lips and also drank from it. Then, she in turn passed the goblet to the man beside her, who similarly drank from it and passed it on.

By now, the man they had sacrificed was dead and a second goblet of his blood had been filled and passed to the priestess, who handed it to the congregation, while a third goblet was being filled.

And so, the Clan drank the fresh red blood. Some drank more neatly than others, who left red rivulets running down from the corners of their mouths; mouths that grinned open to show blood-stained teeth.

While those who had drunk the blood grinned and whooped in delight, the priestess stepped down from the altar with the third goblet in hand and approached her family.

"And we shall all live happily ever after," she told them.

The little girl giggled to her sister and pointed up at the dead man who lay on the altar with a gash in his neck and his skin horribly pallid in the moonlight and torch-glare. " 'cept the sacrifice!" she added in a voice full of childish glee.

"Yeah, sis," her sister agreed with a wise child's nod. "Sacrifice cain't live happily ever after—they're dead!"

***

The next morning after breakfast, Mother called both of her daughters to her and smiled down at them.

"Did you enjoy last night's ceremony, darlings?"

"Oh, yes we did, mamma!" one of them replied.

"Yes! Yes, yes," the other little girl quickly agreed.

Mother, now an everyday wife and mother again and no longer the high priestess, smiled coolly at her daughters. "Remember, my children, that the goddess gives us life. She gives us strength. She give us power! All praise to the goddess!"

"All praise to the goddess!" both daughters loudly proclaimed.

"Oryctolupus—the wolf-rabbit deity," their mother went on. "She without whom our existence is meaningless. And so it has been for generations. So it has been these past three hundred years, in our religion."

The girls nodded enthusiastically.

"And you—you, my children—are our future," Mother said. "Our hopes and the beliefs of the clan lie in you."

Her daughters nodded again, though neither of them really understood what she meant by that.

ACT ONE: ROAD TRIP

CHAPTER 1

15 Years Later

Shirley Wade sat in the one of the offices of the Pittsburgh, PA law firm of McNeil, Jamison and Young, flicking through documents. Occasionally, she'd nod to herself or frown and then mark up one of the documents with her pen.

Shirley, who was twenty-five years old, worked with the firm as a paralegal assistant. She was a very pretty, blue-eyed blonde, with a lovely smile that revealed flashing white teeth.

When Shirley got tired of examining the papers in front of her, she let her gaze stray to the nearby windows through which came both a breeze that moved the gauzy drapes and the sounds of the city. She smiled. This neat and well-situated legal office reassured her. It was a sign that she'd moved up in the world; that her future was bright.

Shirley Wade was a city girl; she'd grown up here in Pittsburgh, though not in these kind of polished surroundings. While her family hadn't exactly been poor, her parents had scrimped both to put food on the table and pay their bills, her dad working at a local steel mill and her mother the dutiful housewife and part-time grocery worker during the occasional layoffs at the mill. Shirley was relieved to have escaped from all of that.

I've a good job now. I'm definitely not about following in mom's footsteps.

Not that Shirley didn't appreciate or respect her mother's sacrifices for she and her siblings. It was just that her mother had gotten married almost immediately she'd left high school, and as such hadn't had any real chance of having a career, like Shirley was having now.

Shirley sighed with relief and returned her attention to her papers.

Oh no, that won't do . . .

Her cellphone rang. She picked it up, grinned at the caller ID, and then, doing her best to suppress a giggle, accepted the call:

"Ted Jamison's office. How may I help you?"

"You know exactly how to help me, Shirley," came the deep masculine reply, and she found herself blushing. The caller was Ted Jamison himself, one of her three bosses here at the law firm, and more importantly, her current fiancée.

"Oh, Ted," she replied, still blushing and desperately hoping that no one would walk into her office now. Ted was 40 years old, darkly handsome, and Shirley simply couldn't get enough of him. They had been dating for two years now and planned to tie the knot around Christmastime.

"You were fantastic last night, sweetheart," Ted said, his voice making her tingle.

Shirley, who wasn't used to speaking so boldly about such things, felt embarrassed. "You were pretty incredible yourself," she replied him in a gentle and seemingly chastened voice, while running her fingers through her hair, unconsciously trying to tidy it as if Ted were there in the room with her, observing her, or was able to see her through the telephone. "But—next time, let's finish up at my place so I can at least change my clothes and get my hair in order. I'm a mess—and it's all your fault, mister."

"My fault? You really mean *pleasure*, don't you, hon. Your pleasure too, I hope. But if it's any consolation, you still look pretty hot, even with the bed head."

Shirley burst into laughter. Ted laughed too, and Shirley felt pleased in the ambit of his love, felt safe and comforted, even though he was only with her at the other end of a phone connection.

Then Ted cleared his throat. "Hey, sweetheart, I wonder if you could do me a favor?"

"Sure," Shirley replied. "What'cha need?"

"There's a FedEx envelope on my desk from Mass Con Energy . . ."

Shirley, feeling a little relieved to be able to shift from flustered fiancée to efficient paralegal again, rose smoothly to her feet. "Okay, give me a second—I'm going through to your office," she said, smoothing down her top with her free hand as she stepped out of her workspace into the connecting corridor. "Yeah?" she said as she walked into an adjacent office. The envelope Ted had mentioned lay on his desk like he'd said.

"Okay, yep, I see the envelope."

"Mass Con Energy . . . Well, they're an oil and gas company needing us to finalize the deal on a tract of land they've bought the mineral rights to . . . in West Virginia. That envelope contains the purchase paperwork. . . . Signed copies of the deeds, to be filed in the Ringo County Courthouse."

Shirley nodded to herself and picked up the package from the desk.

"Okay, so you need me to make copies of this and forward the original to the Ringo County Clerk?"

"Well . . . there's a little more to it than that."

"What's that?"

She heard Ted sigh over the line. "Honey, the title's cloudy. We need to do an extended search. . . . Make sure all bases are covered before they start drilling."

Shirley frowned at that and sat on the edge of Ted's desk, her eyes scanning the law firm's address on the bulky envelope while she said, "Hmm . . . Let me guess—that backwoods county doesn't have their records online, does it?"

"They're still stuck in the 1930s."

"Sounds like a road trip."

Ted laughed. "You catch on quick."

"Okay. . . . So you want me to go all the way over there and check things out. And are you joining me, darling?"

Ted sighed. "We-ell . . . attractive as that sounds . . ."

Shirley giggled and said flirtatiously: "Might be fun. Just the two of us, driving through the mountains . . . and maybe stopping off. . . . You know . . . for a . . . break." In her mind she could see it clearly: Ted veering the bimmer off the highway into the woods and finding them a nice and isolated grove somewhere and then, in that quiet and shadowy spot, surrounded by the gentle chirping of insects and the calls of birds, kissing her and beginning to peel her blouse off.

And Ted clearly saw the same possibilities to their traveling together as she did, because she heard disappointment in his voice when he replied: "Hot damn! I would love to, Shirley, but I have a hearing tomorrow, and I need to prepare for it today. Who knows how long I'll be tied up?"

Shirley couldn't hide her own disappointment. "Oh . . . ."

"And, of course," Ted added, driving a nail into the coffin of her hopes that he'd be able to accompany her to West Virginia, "Mass Con expects their paperwork to be filed ASAP, so we can't postpone it so that I can travel there with you."

"Yes, of course," Shirley quickly agreed, acknowledging that work took a priority here in the office and that romance would have to wait. "Okay. No problem. I can do that, darling."

"So . . . take my car. Heck, you already drove it in to work."

Shirley suppressed a giggle. "Well, Ted, you know I have a thing for cute little bimmers . . . and their owners."

They both burst into laughter at that, and she added: "And besides, my old jalopy might not even make it there. . . . So . . . sure, I'll drive your BMW, since you insist."

"Great. I happy I didn't have to twist your arm too terribly."

"Oh, but I don't do favors for nothing, Ted," Shirley immediately countered. "You owe me big time for this."

"Absolutely! How about I'll take you out to a romantic dinner tonight?"

Shirley grinned at the office windows and the clear blue sky outside. Then she looked back in at the clock on the wall of Ted's office. The time was 8:47 am. "That sounds lovely, but it'll probably be late by the time I get back after this. You know how far away it is. . . . And goodness knows whether they even keep their files in order in Hicksville. It could take me all day just to find the stuff."

"Then, if you're delayed, catch some dinner on the way back and when you get home, we'll just go straight to dessert." He laughed softly. "And, a smart girl like you? I'm sure you know what *dessert* I'm referring to."

Shirley blushed again. Oh yes, she definitely knew what he meant. Just thinking of last night was getting her hot and bothered and so she didn't catch the double entendre in her reply until after she'd said it: "Oh my! I'm pretty hungry myself. I guess I should be leaving right away, then!"

But maybe Ted was too busy then or already had his mind on other things, because while Shirley was starting to feel slightly embarrassed at her sexual innuendo, Ted simply replied: "Thanks, Shirl, you're the best. . . . Sorry, darling, gotta hang up now," and then he did hang up.

Shirley sat there on the edge of his desk for a short while, slowly assembling the stages of her just-assigned road trip in her mind.

Then she got to her feet and returned to her office with the Mass Con Energy envelope in hand. Once she was inside her own office, she began collecting together all the stuff she figured she'd need on her trip down south to West Virginia and Ringo County.

CHAPTER 2

A few hundred miles down south, in the very county (and also exact area of it) that Shirley Wade was destined to shortly arrive in, a man named Roger Alfred was out in the woods hunting.

Roger, a slightly built man in his thirties with dark hair and eyes, walked stealthily through the forest, intend on remaining unheard as he crossed the current grassy clearing he'd reached. His hunting rifle was lowered, but held across his body in a two-handed grip with his right index finger on the trigger, ready to fire in a split second. His body language was relaxed and largely devoid of tension. A casual observer would easily recognize that this wasn't Roger's first time out hunting.

Roger's gaze darted left and right as he walked, alert for the slightest motion. If his body language revealed him to be an experienced hunter, his eyes revealed him to be possibly a mentally unhinged one. His dark eyes held a slightly wild, crazed look in them; the look of a man who'd been shoved one step too far, and was having to deal with consequences previously unforeseen.

He stepped cautiously (and silently) across the clearing grass, his senses alert for danger, for anything out of the ordinary.

He reached the other side of the clearing and slid between the trees there. Disturbed by his arrival, a large squirrel abandoned its lower branch for a higher one. Roger didn't notice the animal's flight. His quarry was near now; he could hear the sound of breaking twigs from a creature that wasn't being anywhere near as careful as he was to go unnoticed. A big creature from the sound of it.

Roger's prey came into view between a pair of maple trees on his right.

With a cold smile on his face, Roger raised his rifle, took careful aim through the sight, and fired off a single shot. There was a single grunt of pain, and next followed the sound of a heavy body hitting the ground.

Roger Alfred smiled a full, wide, sinister smile.

"Gotcha," he whispered with intense pleasure and satisfaction.

CHAPTER 3

Shirley's drive to West Virginia was smooth and easy. Ted's BMW handled like a dream and the miles and lovely countryside streamed pleasantly past Shirley as she drove down out of Pennsylvania.

For a long time, she drove between the Appalachian Mountains, with only the car stereo as her companion. Despite the distance she had to travel, it felt great to be out of the city and on the highway for a while, free as a bird, with empty road and countryside for miles around.

Soon however, the BMW's GPS informed her that she needed to turn off the interstate. And from here on the roads became more 'cramped.' One or two more turnoffs followed, and Shirley needed no tour guide to inform her that she'd now arrived in the backwoods.

Out here the roads were less well maintained, and the relatively prosperous towns she'd previously driven through had now completely given way to isolated single shacks, many of these lying on equally isolated farms. Several of the shacks had the hulks of tireless cars raised on cinderblocks beside them.

"Welcome to the dirt-poor part of the state," Shirley couldn't help remarking aloud as she stopped at a traffic light. What the traffic light was doing out here, she had no idea—she'd not seen another car for five minutes and the black BMW was the only vehicle at the crossroads—but she waited patiently for the light to turn green.

While waiting, she looked around. On her right stood another old shack. This one had a completely rusted tractor parked out front—with blown and cracked tires and the paint all peeled off—beneath which a preschooler (Shirley couldn't determine the kid's gender) was chasing a gray kitten. The kid's mother was hanging up washing a short distance away.

Watching the rustic scene Shirley felt a sudden rush of unease. She couldn't help contrasting the affluence proclaimed by her luxury car with this poverty-stricken, low-income area she was traveling through. She began willing the traffic light to change faster. But no, the damn thing seemed to be taking its sweet time; so much so that she wondered if it was broken and seriously considered driving through the intersection. But then she remembered that it was working; she'd seen it change from green to red right as she was driving up to it. Frustrated, she resumed her wait.

Then a man walked into view on her right, walking past the broke-down tractor, beside which the preschooler—it was a girl—had now caught her kitten and was stroking its mangy fur. The man walked up to the intersection and stepped into the road, onto the crosswalk ahead of her; another incongruity: what did anyone need a crosswalk for in an area this sparsely populated and motored? As he crossed the road, she got a very good look at him. He was dressed in faded brown pants and a faded red shirt that was threadbare at both collar and cuffs. He turned and grinned at her through the windshield and waved. She waved back in disgust. Most of his teeth were gone and those that remained were black lumps. She however realized that even though he looked friendly, his expression also seemed rather bewildered; as if he couldn't for the life of him understand what she was doing out here in the middle of nowhere.

Thankfully, however, he'd soon stepped past the car and she no longer had to look at him, because the light had just turned green again. She quickly put the car in motion and drove off.

However, as she pulled away from the intersection she caught a glimpse of the shabbily dressed man in her rearview mirror. He was standing on the other side of the intersection and staring at her car; she imagined that he still had that same bewildered smile on his face.

His shrinking image gave Shirley a vague sense of unease; but she quickly squashed the feeling. She was here to do a job and she'd soon be done with it and back home again.

CHAPTER 4

Almost at her destination, Shirley pulled over into BIG JIM'S GAS UP, a service station. Ted's fuel gauge was dangerously low now and it wouldn't but that great of a plan to wind up in need of a tow truck.

Totally in keeping with this general area she'd been driving through for the past half-hour, this was an old-style gas station—two miserable looking fuel pumps with a convenience store behind them and a small hut over on the left side of that, beside which stood a battered pickup truck.

She drove in and parked beside the pumps. The pump's metering was digital, but that was about it—fuel station self-service clearly hadn't extended out here yet. And there was no card reader at the pumps.

After waiting a few seconds for someone to come attend to her, Shirley got out of the car and stood staring. *Okay, what do I do now?* The station didn't show any real appearance of life. *But there's a light on in the store, as well as that pickup truck parked over there, so there has to be someone here.*

Feeling rather hesitant, possibly as a carryover from her recent experience with the man at the intersection, Shirley set off for the store.

***

The store interior perfectly matched the general ambience of these backwoods parts. It was rundown and dirty, with scant plastic in evidence. Most of its goods were arranged on wooden shelves. It also had a wooden payment counter and an old-style till. The floor looked like it hadn't been swept in a year. Stepping in through the glass door (the view through which was almost completely obliterated by beer company and energy drink stickers and notices with offers for farm work), Shirley almost felt like she'd stepped into a movie from the thirties. Her wariness about this place was reinforced the moment she saw the attendant.

"Hi, I'm Big Jim," the bald man behind the counter greeted her. He definitely was 'big'—in Shirley's estimation 'Big Jim' must've weighed about three hundred pounds; he had a lot of fat on him.

Big Jim was dressed in a filthy t-shirt shirt and grimy overalls, and was chewing on a smoking cigarette butt, which he now dropped into an out-of-sight ashtray. He seemed to be about forty-five years old and was heavily bearded and tattooed.

Shirley felt deep unease as the man eyes lazily stared her up and down. She tried to speak but at first felt overpowered by his leering scrutiny. She felt like dashing out of the door back to her BMW, leaping into it and driving off. But there was the problem of how long the gas in the car would last. If she drove off in either fright, anger or disgust, there might not be another gas station nearby. She suspected that there *should* be at least one—most likely in the town she was headed for—but felt it was silly to take the chance.

She was relieved to discover that Big Jim had now finished his scrutiny of her body. Now, instead, he nodded towards the grimy store window, beyond which her car was parked at the pump.

"Nice car ya got there," he said in a thankfully businesslike voice. Shirley hadn't come to town to make trouble, but if he'd insisted on being a jerk, she'd have to read him the bill of rights.

"Um . . . thanks," Shirley muttered. "I need to get some high-test gasoline."

"That a rice burner?" Big Jim asked, scratching his bald head with a finger.

"Excuse me?" Shirley had no idea what 'rice-burner' meant. She hoped this nasty man wasn't asking if her car used rice for fuel.

Big Jim seemed to read her confusion. "Your car. Is it one o' those Japanese jobs?"

"Oh. Actually, it's German."

Big Jim grinned at her. He still had most of his teeth, but most of them were as unclean as his person and his premises. "So. Built by Nazis then."

Shirley shuddered at what he was implying about the BMW. "I hope not."

"Ah, nothing wrong with a little Nazi engineering," Big Jim said. "Nazi everything, come to think about it. Efficient and effective, those guys are."

While speaking he stared at Shirley. Then, when he was done staring, he loudly cleared his throat and spat across the counter—not towards her, thankfully—but near one of the metal racks that held old paperbacks and shaving equipment.

Shirley felt dumbfounded. True the phlegm had missed her by a mile, but as she turned and stared at it—a horrible yellow splat on the floor—she felt intense nausea rise up in her.

I just came in here to buy gas! she thought in horror.

She turned back to Big Jim. The large man's eyes were fixed on her intently; indeed so intent was his gaze that she had the impression he was staring into her soul. Despite her attempts to face him down, she recoiled in disgust.

"Gotta respect them Nazis," Big Jim continued with a series of approving nods while scratching his beard. "They did a lotta good stuff, back in the day."

Shirley was now becoming nervous. This sounded like a cliché of every bad thing she'd ever heard about the backwoods.

"So, can I get me some high-test gas?" she said in a cold voice that she hoped didn't sound frightened.

Big Jim shook his head. "Ain't got no high-octane fuel here, lady."

"Oh . . ." Shirley said.

Big Jim laughed with scorn that she wasn't certain wasn't directed towards herself and her so-called 'citified' ways.

"You needn't worry your little ass too much," he said. "Gas is gas. 87 . . . 93 . . . All the same shit, if you ask me."

"Ummm . . . O.K." Now that he'd turned sexist on her with that last 'little ass' comment, she wanted to be well away from his filling station. The sooner she departed from here, the better for her. And this guy Big Jim was apparently a Nazi sympathizer too. She began regretting that there wasn't a gun in the car. She'd feel so much safer if there was.

Big Jim rubbed his bald head with a palm and then gestured out the window again. "Just go ahead and pump. Come back in to pay when you're done."

Relieved to be getting away from the man and his nauseating presence, Shirley nodded and turned away, heading for the door. But just when she'd gotten the door open, he called out to her: "Bend over deep while you're pumping, sweet cheeks, and I might even give ya the Big Jim discount."

He burst out laughing, while Shirley froze at the door, not quite believing what she'd heard. He kept laughing however, and his mirth seemed to propel her out of the convenience store and back into the world outside.

Deciding that the sooner she got this over with the better for her, she walked towards the gas pumps, now unconsciously gripping her bunch of keys with their jagged ends poking out between the fingers of her closed fist, like a weapon.

Shirley pumped her gas and paid for it, while Big Jim continued to ogle her and make crude sexual innuendos. He truly was a pig and a stereotypical representative of everything bad she'd ever heard about the backwoods.

She found it impossible to quantify her relief when she left the convenience store for the second time.

Welcome to the country, she though grimly, as she climbed into the BMW and drove off.

CHAPTER 5

Inside the Respite Motor Lodge, Roger Alfred was on the phone to his mother.

Phone receiver held to his ear, Roger was standing behind the reception desk, waiting for clients. Outside, the rusted motel sign swung in the wind, and since he could both see it through the front windows of the reception hall and occasionally even hear it creaking and banging against its pole, it distracted him.

Roger readily admitted that the establishment was run down; it needed lots of renovation, including several fresh coats of paint.

At the moment, the Respite wasn't exactly doing lots of business. Sure, the area's general impoverishment contributed to that, but Roger also knew that merely 'judging a book by its cover' as it were, was certain to encourage visitors to the town to look elsewhere for accommodation.

His eyes roved over the small and currently empty reception area, while he mentally assessed just how much it would cost to upgrade both the building's interior and exterior. Those sagging chairs in the corner, for instance, would most definitely be thrown out once he had the funds to replace them.

While estimating the cost of renovation and repairs, he kept up his phone conversation, saying: "Aw, come on, maw. Mind the desk. Just for a couple of hours."

Roger listened to his mother's voice. The old woman was asking where'd he'd been earlier in the day. "Hunting, maw. Killed some more," he replied.

He listened again, nodded to himself and frowned.

"Oh, it went well—just like you said it would. I know! I know it was only this morning, but I got a taste for it, now." The thrill of the morning's kill still filled Roger and he felt desperate to leave his current post—this humdrum receptionist assignment of waiting for no one to check in—and head out into the woods again.

He chuckled into the phone receiver. "I mean it, maw—right now I'm in a mood to go huntin' again. Blood-lust, you might say. So, you just please come on over and mind the front desk for a couple hours and I'll be on my merry way. It's quiet here. Quiet as death. You'll have nothing to do." He paused, listening to her muted reply, and then added: "Besides, you like what I bring back from my hunting trips, don't you?"

Roger paused again, listened to what his mother was saying, and then his thin lips broke into a broad grin. "You will? Maw, you're the best! Sure. I'll just be here, waitin' . . . cleanin' my weapon. Just gettin' myself ready."

Roger put down the phone and smiled broadly to himself; a shadow of craziness once more falling on his face.

CHAPTER 6

Even though that sexist pig Big Jim was thankfully miles behind her now, Shirley still felt stressed.

"Dammit how much further to go is there?" she growled at the GPS, while the device stolidly remained quiet and its visuals remained unerringly indicating that she continue on her current course.

The problem was that to the left and right of her everywhere looked much the same; old shacks, cultivated or abandoned farmland, woodland, and yet the town she was certain should be out here and which the GPS assured *was* out here, was still nowhere in sight.

She glanced down at her watch, hoping that the damn GPS wasn't busted and she wouldn't have to backtrack and begin asking folks for direction, then huffed out a frustrated breath. Then she made a right curve through a thickly wooded corner and . . .

Like magic—as if it had appeared just for her—she saw a town in the distance.

"Come on . . . come on!" she growled as she slowed a little and squinted to read the road sign she was now approaching.

The road sign read:

'WELCOME TO WILLIAMSON, COUNTY SEAT OF RINGO COUNTY.'

Shirley heaved a deep sign of relief. "Here at last," she told herself.

***

Now once more following the GPS's directions with confidence, Shirley drove the BMW through the town of Williamson. The town was a medium-sized place, not exactly as rundown and hickish as its outskirts had led her to expect, but not exactly prosperous-looking either. Though most of the buildings were in good repair, most also looked like they could do with fresh paintjobs.

To Shirley's mind the whole place had a griminess to it that she detested. But she quickly shook that impression off:

This is just a decent town filled with decent folks, she told herself as she arrived at the county courthouse. *I need to watch myself and not act prejudiced and superior. I'm just still bummed about my bad experience back at the gas station.*

Shirley drove slowly towards the courthouse, looking for a vacant parking spot. A large proportion of the vehicles parked around the courthouse building were pickup trucks. She figured that made sense, seeing as farming seemed to be the primary occupation around here.

She found a vacant parking space near the main courthouse entrance.

She pulled into one free slot and sat for a few moments collecting her thoughts. She glanced out through the window on her side to make sure she wasn't too close to the parking meter, and then feeling hot and bothered, looked at her watch. The time was now 2:28 pm, meaning she'd spent over five hours in transit from Pittsburgh.

She exhaled a deep breath: "Crap. It's so late!"

She got out her phone and swiped on the screen, then she tapped on through to phone contacts. Ted's name was first on her list of recent calls. She called him and waited, then realized that her call wasn't going through. She tried calling Ted again and then, when she once more couldn't connect, examined the screen more carefully.

"No service?" she grimaced. "Shit."

Suddenly she felt really disgusted. In this day and age were there really such places as this, places where the latest joys of civilization hadn't penetrated to? She looked around at her surroundings, at the quiet and seemingly subdued (in her mind at least) townsfolk as they walked or drove along the street.

"Wow, what a one-horse town this is," she grumbled. "Well, it would be if it had a horse!"

A sense of urgency now gripped Shirley. Realizing that she had quite a lot to do and that time really wasn't on her side here, she grabbed her purse and got out of her car. Meaning to simply feed the parking meter before picking up the legal documents she'd brought along with her, she left the car door open.

Now she paid proper to the parking meter and sighed. It was as old-fashioned as the town it stood in. The 'expired' flag was showing.

She began rummaging through her purse frantically, looking for change.

"Dammit, dammit," she cursed under her breath as she shifted around the purse's contents and realized she had no change to feed the parking meter.

Oh, screw it, they can ticket me, she finally decided.

This decision reached, Shirley leaned into the BMW and grabbed up her attaché case containing the Mass Conn folder from the passenger seat. Then she slammed the door, locked it, and rushed into the courthouse.

Maybe it was because she was still feeling flustered on her arrival in town, but one thing Shirley Wade hadn't noticed was that she'd parked her car rather haphazardly, halfway across a regular parking space and just over the line into a handicapped slot.

CHAPTER 7

Inside the old courthouse, Shirley's enquiries quickly led her to a large but plain room in the rear of the building, which along with scores of bookcases, was furnished with several tables and chairs like a library. Two men in suits sat at different tables looking through files.

The county records service desk was manned by a serious-looking young brunette.

"Yes, I think you'll find what you need in here, ma'am," she said in response to Shirley's queries concerning the title deeds that related to Mass Con Energy's land purchases. "The records here extend pretty far back, some of them as far back as the nineteenth century even."

Shirley nodded. The records keeper was a pretty but mousy girl. Shirley assumed the young woman was a few years younger than herself. She was dressed very conservatively, in a dull gray dress, and also wore very unfashionable glasses.

Shirley gestured over at the records, and then giggled nervously. "Wow, there's so damn many of them," she said. "Where do I start looking?"

The brunette nodded back at her without smiling. She didn't strike Shirley as being deliberately unfriendly; a slight frostiness just seemed to be a part of her natural demeanor. "Yes, the amount of documents stored here can seem overwhelming," she agreed. She gestured at the folder Shirley was holding. "Let me see the deed and I'll be able to direct you."

Shirley quickly got the relevant document out of her folder and handed it over.

The young woman scanned the paper for a few seconds, tapping it with plain fingernails, while her lips tightened in concentration. Then she frowned up at Shirley. "Oh, no problem. The papers you'll be looking for are right over there."

Shirley followed her pointing finger. "Okay, but which one of them is it?"

"Come with me," she said, stepping out from behind her desk. Her black shoes were as plain and unfashionable as her clothes.

She led Shirley across the room to one of the further bookcases and began scanning the spines of the large tomes it contained.

"Yeah, here it is," she said finally, and pulled out an especially large volume from a middle shelf, which she then carried before Shirley to a nearby table and opened up for her.

"Thanks," Shirley said as she turned to leave. "I think I'll be okay now."

The woman nodded. "It's what I'm here for. Please let me know if you need anything else."

She walked off and Shirley settled down to read, but not before noting that the hands of the old-fashioned clock on the wall (wasn't anything modern in this town?) showed the time to be 2:45pm.

Not too bad, she thought as she began to turn the pages with concentration. *If I'm lucky, this shouldn't take me more than an hour or an hour-and-a-half to resolve, and then I can drive out of here back to civilization again. What kind of a backwards town doesn't have a cellphone connection in this day and age?*

CHAPTER 8

Free from the tyranny of the motel (as he now thought of it) Roger was once again out stalking prey in the woods.

At the moment he was walking just inside the tree line on the outskirts of Williamson but intended to penetrate deeper amongst the trees.

He was being cautious, however; it wouldn't do for anyone to realize that he was responsible for what had been happening out here. And for that reason, he'd parked his pickup truck a good quarter mile down the highway (and on the other side of the road) and then doubled back down this way to start his hunting.

He had a good feel about today. This morning's hunt had yielded a fine prize of death. And Roger, his eyes gleaming brightly with something like madness now, had no doubt that this afternoon's proceedings would turn out to be just as fruitful—if not more so, even.

The one difference from this morning's business in the woods was that this time Roger was hunting with a crossbow.

The crossbow was lighter and also silent—but just as deadly if used right. And Roger didn't plan to miss hitting what he was aiming at anyway. The crossbow was loaded and primed and even though it currently dangled down by Roger's right leg, it would be the work of mere seconds to sweep it up and send its cargo of death streaking through the air.

Roger's gaze scoured the area, his every sense alert, both for the prey he sought and for other eyes that might be observing him too.

He moved on, once more stepping silently, as quiet as a wolf tracking a rabbit.

And then, suddenly, he heard it. A sound like a laugh or an animal noise. He froze in his tracks and his lips parted in a broad smile.

This was too easy; he felt like laughing.

He cocked his head like a dog to hear better. The sound vanished for a few seconds. But then it came again, slightly louder this time and he noted exactly from what direction it had come—not directly ahead as he'd imagined the first time he'd heard it, but over on his left, towards the south.

Roger smiled to himself. "Well, I'm a comin' to git ya!"

Now raising the crossbow to a firing position, he moved forward, silently as always, through the trees again.

Soon he was in range and could see his target.

***

Across from Roger, and standing in the dappled shade at the edge of a small clearing, a young couple were balanced against a tree. The young woman had her back to the tree. The young man had his pants down around his ankles and the woman's skirt was raised up over her waist as he kissed her.

Roger nodded at the couple and then smirked.

The young woman broke off the kiss and began giggling, causing her blonde hair to whip across her shoulders. Her lover pushed up against her and fondled her.

The young woman bit her lip, smiling and enjoying his touch as he moved against her and inside of her. Then she began panting.

Roger took careful aim at his targets. This was going to be a tricky shot, but he thought he'd be able to make it.

Across from Roger, and both completely unaware of the scent of death in the air nearby, the young couple continued making love against the tree. The young man began groaning now in rhythm with his thrusts. His blonde partner began moaning also.

And then there was a sudden 'Thwunk!' sound. A loud noise completely out of place in either the couple erotic delights or the pleasant afternoon forest.

The young man grunted one final time, extra loudly. The young woman's blue eyes widened, and she groaned; but hers wasn't a groan of pleasure but one of agony.

Blood started to trickle from the sides of the girl's mouth.

Leaving his place of concealment among the trees, Roger dashed across the clearing towards them, his eyes wide in amazement. He'd have been doing a rebel yell if he could, but this wasn't the South.

"Well, I'll be damned!" Roger exclaimed as he reached the couple, who were still standing up against the tree.

But neither of the lovers could reply. Roger knew they couldn't reply him. The only reason the young man and his girlfriend were standing upright now was that they'd been pinned to the tree by the crossbow bolt that Roger had shot through both of their bodies. The sturdy metal shaft now fastened the two of them together, tight against the tree, their arms hanging limp by their sides. Both of their heads hung downwards as if there was something of intense importance on the ground that they needed to study.

So, no, Roger hadn't been expecting any kind of a reply or even surprise from the copulating couple. His glee and amazement now was due entirely to the fact that he'd gotten the shot right first time.

He felt ecstatic. "You shoot your bolt, boy? Hey?" he asked the motionless young man. "Hell yeah! Me, too!"

Then he gripped the young man's dark hair and lifted his head and turned the kid's face towards him for a better look, nodding in satisfaction at the glazed eyes and the stream of blood running from his mouth. He didn't bother examining the girl; she was clearly just as dead as the boy was, the crossbow bolt having penetrated her heart.

Roger slapped his thighs in intense mirth. "Yessir, I got me two for the price of one! Who'd a thunk it? Wait till I tell maw 'bout this!"

His laughter filled the forest clearing.

CHAPTER 9

Shirley's research went well; most of the information she needed was readily available in the volume the clerk had found for her.

There was simply a lot of it to get through, pages to request photocopies of and others she merely scanned with her cellphone—it was still good for that at least.

Once, when Shirley needed additional information to cross-reference and confirm a few murky details about past land transactions regarding Mass Con Energy's newly-purchased property, she got up and searched the relevant bookcase herself. She did consider asking the woman at the desk for her assistance, but at that point in time the serious and bespectacled brunette was attending to two young women, and her frown dissuaded Shirley from bothering her.

Thankfully, her personal search yielded fast results. She returned to her study table with two additional volumes, and was soon once more lost in her work.

With books open on the table and documents spread out, Shirley buried herself in her task, unconscious of the passage of time.

Then—"Ma'am," a voice interrupted her flow of thought.

Shirley was startled. Despite having been aware of approaching footsteps, she'd assumed someone was about walking past her. She looked up and saw that it was the brunette records keeper.

"Yes?" she asked, barely concealing her irritation at having her concentration broken.

"Ma'am, we are getting ready to close," the woman said.

Shirley looked across at the old-fashioned timepiece on the wall. It showed the hour as four o'clock on the dot. She was surprised at how time had flown while she'd been busy. "You're kidding me . . . I thought you stayed open until five?"

The young woman shook her head. "No. We close at four p.m. If you haven't finished with what you were researching, you'll need to come back tomorrow."

"I just need a little while longer," Shirley replied. "I'm almost finished. Give me a few minutes more."

Without waiting to hear the other woman's response, she immediately turned back to reading. She figured her frosty companion would need to attend to a few matters before she could legitimately kick her out. However, she'd clearly been telling the truth about her department's closing time. Two tables away from Shirley, a young man who'd been crosschecking a set of ancient blueprints was busy rolling them up.

Shirley hadn't even begun working again when she felt a gentle tap on her shoulder. The pressure of female fingers was insistent and meaningful; not something she could ignore.

She turned to look at the brunette again. The young woman was staring at her over the top of her glasses; and Shirley imagined that now she saw a trace of menace in her eyes.

"You will be sure to put the books back where you found them now, won't you, ma'am? I'd really appreciate that. We can't have things in disarray here."

Shirley pulled back from her, frowning. There was something about the girl's touch that felt . . . unhealthy.

She nodded. "Okay, I get the message. Of course. I'll put them away. Like I said, I'm just about finished anyway . . . just rechecking a few final details."

Smiling coldly, the attendant nodded back at Shirley. "You can have ten minutes more in here, but then I really do need to lock up."

"Thanks," Shirley said.

Once the girl had left her, she busied herself with finalizing her day's work.

CHAPTER 10

Shirley left the courthouse feeling satisfied. Despite the young clerk's frostiness, she'd accomplished what she came here for.

All I need to do now is find somewhere to have a late lunch and then drive back home and have a cool bath . . . and then I'll relax and let Ted pamper me . . .

But, immediately on stepping outside of the courthouse into its front parking lot, she saw that something was amiss. She pulled up short and stared.

Her car—actually Ted's car—was missing.

"What?"

She looked around in confusion, but there was no doubt about it. The space where her car had been parked was empty.

Shirley stared back at the vacant parking space as if willing the car to reappear. "What the hell?"

She stood there, looking up and down the street in bewilderment, first trying to convince herself that maybe she'd forgotten where she'd parked, and next wondering if maybe she'd accidentally left the building by a different route from that by which she'd entered it; if maybe she had mistaken one of courthouses entrances/exits for another. But no, she was finally forced to admit, this was the way she'd come in; she was certain of it.

Once Shirley had settled in her mind that she was standing at the right exit, she got out her cell phone, thinking to call either Ted or the police.

She winced at the "No Service" message on the phone's screen. "Dammit to hell!" she growled and violently shoved the device back into her purse again.

She felt bewildered as she examined the faces of the passing townsfolk, several of whom quickened their step and hurried past the courthouse when they noticed her wild stare. And indeed, at that moment, Shirley Wade did seem a little crazy to those unenlightened as to her current plight.

She couldn't grasp what had happened to her car. *Was the BMW stolen outside the county courthouse? Can that even happen? That doesn't seem possible!*

She looked desperately around, flustered and uncertain what to do next. *Oh, damn, Ted is gonna be so pissed off about this! He loves that car!*

Then she sensed motion behind her and spun around. She relaxed somewhat on noticing the shady-looking figure shambling towards her. Judging from the way he was dressed, the man was a homeless person or a bum. From his lurching gait, he might even be drunk.

She decided to get out of his way and let him pass her by, but then his eyes locked on hers and she realized she was his target; so she waited. He couldn't attack her in broad daylight in front of the courthouse with townsfolk walking about to witness everything, could he?

But that's what I assumed about Ted's bimmer too!

"Lookin' fur yer car?" the bum asked her, and with his words came the stink of the unwashed. His face was grimy, his fingernails dirty and his clothes were two degrees short of falling apart on his back. One of his scuffed canvas sneakers was ripped open on the side, showing toenails as dirty as his fingernails.

Concealing her disgust, Shirley nodded back at him. "Do you know what happened to my car? Did you see who stole it?"

The bum shook his head emphatically. "Nobody stole nuttin'. Yuz parked in the crippled space. Sheriff had ya towed."

Crippled space? Oh, he means disabled parking—the handicapped spot! But . . . towed?

Shirley stared at the man open-mouthed, then shook her head and frowned in disbelief. "You must be shitting me!"

The bum shook his head. "Naw . . . I ain't shittin' ya. Happens all the time." He gestured back up at the courthouse. "But you might wanna get back to the sheriff's office before they close."

He stepped closer to Shirley, and in the light of the evening sun she saw his facial features intimately; the smudged face with its untrimmed beard and mustache, the stained teeth and the red eyes. His breath reeked of stale food.

He was still speaking to her: "If yer lucky, miz, maybe yuz get it 'fore it leaves town. Once yer car's in the impound, ya might as well kiss it bye-bye."

As if demonstrating her car leaving her for good, the bum blew her a smelly kiss. Shirley reflexively stepped back from him and then looked around helplessly.

The bum shambled off then, trudging his shabby presence down the road.

"Son-of-a-bitch," Shirley said to herself as she watched him go. She wasn't cussing the departing man, who'd actually helped her, but rather this absurd situation she'd unwittingly gotten herself into.

Then she turned around and hurried back into the courthouse.

CHAPTER 11

Shirley had already passed by the sheriff's office in the courthouse twice today and so had no difficulty locating it again now. The office was located on the left along the main courthouse corridor, just before the turn into the corridor that led to the records office.

Shirley was very conscious of time passing as she hurried to the sheriff's door. Once there, she grasped the doorknob and tried to turn it.

"Oh, dammit!" she cussed on realizing that the door was locked. The top half of the door was glass, and looking in through it, Shirley saw that the sheriff's office was deserted, its lights all turned off; the interior in shadow.

Clearly the town's lawman had left for the day too.

She stood there in the corridor wondering what to do. *Here I am in this no-horse town, with my car towed and no cellphone connection. I guess the smart thing to do is find a landline somewhere and place a call to the office in Pittsburgh and let Ted know I'm stranded here.*

Then she heard footsteps approaching behind her and turned around to see who was coming.

It was the young brunette clerk from the records office. Apparently, she'd just gotten through with locking up the place. She looked smart (if still unsophisticated) with her beige jacket on and her purse slung over her shoulder. She also seemed more human now that she wasn't behind her desk, shepherdess of the town's archaic records.

The young woman smiled coolly on noticing Shirley standing by the sheriff's door. "Sheriff's gone for the day," she said. "Just like me, everyone leaves around 4:00."

"Crap!" Shirley said, looking, sounding, and feeling desperate. "I think they towed my car," she explained to the girl.

"Awww. That sucks," the girl replied sympathetically. "But maybe tomorrow, when they're open, you can stop by and see him."

She started to walk past Shirley, but then stopped and looked at her curiously.

"I don't know what I'm going to do," Shirley said desperately.

"Hmmm," the girl said. "Wish I could help, but . . ."

Shirley looked up and down the corridor, her face distraught. Then she realized that the brunette girl was still staring at her; and that now she had a thoughtful look on her face.

"Hey, would you like me to give you a ride to your house? I'm April, by the way."

She extended a hand in greeting. Shirley shook it even though her mind wasn't really on the physical contact, and so she didn't think of giving her own name in exchange. She was so distracted now that she also missed the opportunity to either reinforce or dismiss her earlier impression of the unpleasantness of the young clerk's touch.

"Thank you, that's kind of you," she said though, with a soft laugh. "But I live almost five hours away from here."

The brunette—April—raised an eyebrow.

"Yeah, I know," Shirley continued. "I'm so screwed! There's no cell phone service . . . I don't have a car and I don't even know where the closest hotel is."

April smiled a little frostily. "There aren't any hotels or motels nearby . . . None that I'd recommend, anyway. There's that old motor lodge – The Respite – on Route 52, but you'd likely get bed bugs if you stayed there."

Shirley grimaced and then shrugged. "Well, I'm really not a big fan of bedbugs, but if that's my only choice—"

"So . . . hmmm . . . well.," April went on. "This is a bit crazy for me, but I've watched you studying for three hours and you seem okay."

She paused and peered searchingly into Shirley's eyes. In those few moments, before April resumed speaking, Shirley had an impression like she was being cross-examined in court.

"So . . . I don't usually do this kind of thing," April went on, "but you look pretty normal . . . You *are* normal, right?"

Shirley smiled back at her: "Well, that depends. Some may say I'm not." Then she grinned broadly. "But I'm not a serial killer, if that's what you mean!"

They both laughed at that response.

"Of course not!," April quickly agreed. "You're more like me. Normal. And I trust my instincts. Okay. Anyway, I have an idea. How about you stay the night at my place, and we can ride back here together in the morning, when I come in to work?"

Their shared laughter had loosened the ice between them somewhat and also made Shirley feel just a little bit better about her current straits; but she still didn't wish to impose on a stranger if she could help it.

"Oh, you're very kind," she said. "But . . . I really don't want to impose . . ."

"Oh, for gosh sakes," April said. "It's no trouble. Not as much as bedbugs would be . . ."

Shirley ran her hand through her hair, and her expression turned thoughtful.

"Well . . ." she said indecisively, "I guess . . ."

"Look, I'm not going to beg," April said in some impatience. "But you won't get a better offer. Not around here."

Shirley sighed. "Well, if you really don't mind. . . . But . . . I wouldn't expect you to do this. I mean—if I could even get to a crummy motel, I would be grateful."

April sighed too. "Up to you. I can drop you off at the motel, but you'd still be stuck there tomorrow with no transport. Or—if you come home with me, I can give you a ride in, easy."

"Well, if you do put me up for the night, I'll be happy to pay you."

But April shook her head emphatically at the offer of payment. "Hogwash! I'm glad I can help. Although . . . I can easily drive you to the motel if you would rather."

"Oh, I don't know."

"It's a few miles out, though. But still . . . You might prefer it to a strange woman driving you off into the unknown!"

Shirley shrugged. She still felt uncertain. Even though she would most definitely prefer staying the night at April's place to an impersonal and bedbug-ridden motel room, she couldn't help but be on her guard. Something about this girl April bothered her.

April was still speaking, and now she laughed. ". . . I mean, we've all watched those horror films . . . right?"

Shirley smiled uneasily. "Hmmm. . . . Crazy motel managers and all. Bit of a cliché, though, isn't it?"

That statement seemed to strike April as funny, because she grinned. "Choice is yours!" she said. "And this guy at the motel I'll be taking you to even *looks* like Norman Bates . . . . plus, he lives with his mother—who's more unseen than not."

Shirley nodded and smiled. "Oh, alright. You've convinced me; let's go to your place then."

"Follow me," April said and led the way out of the courthouse again to where she'd parked her car.

CHAPTER 12

If one was familiar with the term 'automobile graveyard,' the Ringo County Impound Yard definitely fit that description.

Surrounded by deep, thick woods and enclosed by a chain-link fence, the impound yard appeared to extend for miles and miles. In reality it was much smaller, of course, but yet had a sense of disorganization to its layout that could leave one feeling lost and helpless as one made one's way between the rows of parked cars, stripped car husks and the piles of dismantled automobiles parts that made the impound yard also seem like a junkyard.

The sole access route to the Ringo County impound yard was a dirt road, a turnoff from Route 14, a few miles out of Williamson town.

With Shirley Wade's black BMW in tow behind it, a tow truck rolled down that dirt road towards the front gate of the impound yard.

The tow truck's owner/driver was Leroy Sangras, a slim weasley man with straggly black rocker-length hair and a thin mustache. As the truck neared the impound entrance, Leroy took a tattooed hand off of the steering wheel and scratched the crotch of his faded overalls. Then he grinned at the armed guard on duty at the impound gate, who grinned back and immediately waved him on through.

Leroy whistled a country tune to himself as he drove down one of the impound's side driveways, to where there was space available to park the BMW.

Once there, he parked and got out of his truck. He didn't attempt to disengage the BMW, but instead walked over to the large garage on the far side of the space, up against the compound's east wall.

Leroy considered yelling to announce his presence; but the man he wanted to see had clearly already heard him pull up outside. This wasn't always the case of course; Buffalo might've been napping, or even entertaining a woman in the garage.

William "Buffalo" Springfield stepped out of the garage entrance, flicking ash off of his cigarette. Buffalo was a bearded and mustached lumberjack-looking man, dressed in grease-smeared denim pants and an army jacket; he looked mean as a hungry pitbull. After squinting up at the sun, Buffalo flexed his large biceps and frowned at Leroy.

"Hey, whatcha got for us, Leroy?"

"Black BMW," Leroy replied. "Classy vehicle—top of the range. Should fetch us a pretty penny. You know how much they sell these foreign jobs for."

Buffalo walked closer to the tow truck, then around to the back of it to get a good look at the fresh merchandise Leroy had towed in. He appraised the black BMW with an expert eye and nodded in satisfaction. "Yeah I do," he agreed. "Did you get it from downtown?"

Leroy nodded. "Affirmative. T-Bird called it in."

Buffalo grimaced on hearing that. "Well . . . no getting away from it. I suppose our esteemed Sheriff will want his cut, then."

"Affirmative to that as well," Leroy agreed. "He expects his cut right away, for fetching such a great prize." Leroy cocked his head sideways and then jerked a thumb back towards the yard entrance. "In fact, lest my ears is deceiving me, that's him comin' in now—he was tailing me all the way here."

Buffalo looked over the way Leroy was indicating and saw that the man hadn't been exaggerating. A police cruiser had just turned the far end of the aisle of parked vehicles they stood in and was heading towards them.

Buffalo laughed. "What? Sheriff don't trust us? He thinks we're criminals?"

He dropped his cigarette to the ground and stamped it out. Then he and Leroy both silently watched the sheriff's car draw nearer, till finally it parked right next to Leroy's tow truck.

Sheriff Thomas Bird (aka T-Bird to most folks in Ringo County) got out of his police cruiser and grinned at the two men. Sheriff T-Bird was an imposing man: clean cut, slightly overweight and with an arrogant look to him. He was still wearing his uniform; which Leroy and Buffalo both realized meant that the sheriff hadn't been home yet; he'd been in too much of a hurry to discuss the business at hand first.

"Gentlemen!" T-Bird greeted heartily, slapping his hand against the butt of the service revolver holstered at his waist.

Leroy stepped aside as the sheriff strode forward. Sure, they were all criminals here, but Leroy wasn't as far up the pecking order as Buffalo. Also, the sheriff made Leroy slightly uneasy. Best to let Buffalo deal with him.

And true to type Buffalo was already taking the initiative. "Sheriff Thomas Bird, as I live and breathe!" he said in a saccharine and very insincere voice. "What a pleasant and unexpected surprise."

The sheriff wasn't taken in one bit. "Yeah, Buffalo, whatever," he grunted back. Then he gestured towards the BMW. "Ain't she a real beauty?"

While stroking his mustache, Buffalo acted like he didn't understand the question: "Now, which of your daughters are you talkin' about? Cos they are both damn fine-lookin' girls."

T-Bird scowled at him, tapping his holster with his hand. "And I am wearing my loaded gun. You just remember that."

"He's just joshing with ya, T-Bird," Leroy said quickly to defuse any tension that might arise from Buffalo's rash statement. Everyone knew how protective the sheriff was of his daughters. Leroy didn't like the way T-Bird was looking at Buffalo now, speculatively like . . . like he'd like to catch him foolin' with one of his girls and shoot him in the nuts.

To get everybody back on the same page again, Leroy rapped his knuckles on the hood of the BMW. "But, yeah, what a beaut! Know whose it was?"

T-Bird shrugged dismissively, and shifted his weight from his right foot to his left. "Some tourist or other. Don't matter."

Leroy nodded. "Nope. Don't matter at all. The inconsiderate asshole left it parked in the handicapped zone. So, by all illegal rights it's ours now."

That defused any leftover tension between the sheriff and Buffalo. They all laughed at the car owner's misfortune.

"So, down to business," T-Bird said when their amusement had run its course. He dipped his hands into his waistband and hitched his pants up, and then asked: "What's she worth?"

Once more Buffalo feigned ignorance. Leroy hoped he wasn't going to crack another joke about T-Bird's kids. But then, with brow wrinkled in thought, Buffalo asked: "What's *she* worth? You mean the car? Or the tourist?"

The question cracked them all up again.

"Oh, I think we all know the answer to that one, boys," T-Bird said when their laughter had subsided again.

"We sure do," Buffalo and Leroy both agreed sagely.

The three men got down to discussing exactly how to dispose of the black BMW and who got what percentage of the profits from the sale.

CHAPTER 13

April lived well outside of town. That much quickly became apparent to Shirley.

April's car was a relatively new Kia hatchback, and she drove cautiously enough, but the longer the journey took, and the longer they remained on this dirt road seemingly in the middle of nowhere that they'd turned onto a short distance outside of Williamson (and that after having left the town by a different route from that by which Shirley had driven into the place), the more Shirley wondered how in the world April's car hadn't fallen to pieces ages ago. The road was that rural, unsurfaced and dusty, and was bordered in turn by forest, then untended farmland, then by cornfields and hayfields until finally they drove through a pig farm with a large building in the background.

Shirley kept her revulsion from showing as April wheeled them past a set of hog pens, with the smell of the animals spilling thickly into the car.

The road was potholed here and so April slowed the car down, which afforded Shirley a peek into two of the closer pig pens on the right side of the road. The hogs lay there snuffling happily in the mud; amongst them a sow with a litter of squealing piglets; and while the piglets nuzzled their mothers milk-distended teats, the sow in turn was eating something that looked like a mess of meat and rags, like someone had dropped their shirt in a meat grinder, which Shirley, who was doing her best to hold her breath until April navigated this unpleasant patch of road, assumed might actually occur on a rural pig farm like this. Yes, that was clearly what had happened, she decided on catching a brief glimpse of a another hog nudging the arm of an old shirt through the mud.

But then they were past the pigs and thankfully their smell receded with their pens. Not much though, but sufficiently that Shirley dared breathe again as April pulled up to an old farmhouse around the corner from the pig pens.

Shirley did a double-take. The two-storey house was very ramshackle-looking. It was almost in as much disrepair as the shacks she had passed earlier on her drive into town.

April was already getting out of the car, and Shirley had no choice but to follow her lead.

"We're here! Home sweet home!" April said enthusiastically, gesturing at the farmhouse.

Shirley looked around in puzzlement. She didn't wish to be either rude or offensive, but still, she couldn't help her next remark: "Oh. This isn't what I expected your place to be like . . ."

April had begun walking towards the house, but now she stopped for a moment and laughed good-naturedly. "C'mon now, what in the world were you expecting? That I lived in a New York loft apartment? No. I still live here in my mamma and pappy's place."

Shirley nodded. "Oh, I didn't mean any offense by what I said. I'm sorry, I think my mind's still in the city. Today is just turning out so strange, that's all."

She didn't tell April the real cause of her disappointment. It wasn't so much the building that was upsetting her, but her growing suspicion as she regarded the dilapidated old farmhouse that there might not be a landline in there from which she could call her boyfriend Ted and tell him of this awkward situation in which she had found herself.

But, considering his beloved bimmer was at stake here (if the bum she'd met outside the courthouse was to be believed) maybe the current lack of modern telecommunications was a blessing in disguise.

She was relieved to see that her companion hadn't taken any offense at her unkind and unguarded utterance. April just smiled understandingly, took off her glasses and polished them on her sleeve.

"Hey, pappy won't be back for a little while," she said, replacing her glasses on the bridge of her nose again. "And mamma is—well, I'll need to explain about her . . . before you meet her. But first, how about we go meet my sister May? She's usually in the woodshed with her hides."

Shirley stared at her in confusion. "Hides?"

April nodded. "Yeah. Hides—you know—animals' skins. May's a trapper and makes all kinds of cool stuff. You name it—hats, purses . . . lucky rabbit's feet . . ." She laughed. "Of course, I guess it wasn't too lucky for the rabbits, huh?"

Then she grinned impishly at Shirley, surprising Shirley because she now seemed an entirely different personality from the serious young lady who worked at the town records office.

"C'mon then," she said, gesturing to Shirley to follow her. "Let's go find my sis!"

She set off walking along the side of the farmhouse and Shirley followed her around the building's far corner.

There was a woodshed at the back of the house, which was where April led Shirley to.

CHAPTER 14

For Shirley, stepping inside the woodshed was like entering a strange, new, and unsettling world. Though she guessed a tanner's workplace would, out of necessity look something like this, the place seemed macabre to her. Animal skins of varying kinds were strung up on cross-wise lines and stretched across wooden pegs fixed to the rough wooden walls; then there were all the jars of chemicals arranged on shelves as well as additional jars of unknown substances on the floor and worktables. Various tools were arrayed on the shed's work surfaces, miscellaneous bladed implements that Shirley thought looked alarmingly sharp.

And then there was the smell to contend with. It hit Shirley the moment she stepped in through the door, a thick and blended odor of various animal musks that was further mingled with a chemical tinge, a smell that was almost like that of a hospital, but was then further corrupted by the slightly nauseating smell of blood; both fresh and old blood. Shirley tried to hide the fact that she was almost gagging for breath. The smell of the pig pens had been upsetting too; but that had been a stench of life; in here there was only the smell of death; both new and old death.

At one of the worktables a young woman sat, head down, eyes focused in concentration, cleaning a fur with a knife. April's sister May was a gorgeous and voluptuous woman. That impression struck Shirley immediately she set her eyes on her.

She stole a glance at her companion. *She's sort of like April . . . if April was less formal in her dressing; April dresses with the utmost seriousness.* The sisters' bone structure was similar—a single glance at their faces would leave no doubt about the blood connection between them—but . . . May seemed to be April's polar opposite. For one thing, she seemed to have better (as in more modern) fashion sense. She had long purple hair and was wearing a bikini top, Daisy Dukes and cowboy boots.

She looked lost in concentration as she scraped her animal skin clean.

"Hey, sis," April said by way of greeting.

May looked up in surprise and then relaxed. Then she stared Shirley up and down. Her gaze seemed both curious and mildly amused.

"Yo-yo-domino. Who's the chick?" she asked. Her voice had the same timbre as April's but once again, it was looser; indicative of a more relaxed personality.

Shirley saw that April was staring inquisitively at her. "Um . . . I don't believe I caught your name," she said.

Which made Shirley recall that she'd not introduced herself back at the courthouse; she'd been too distracted by the disappearance of her car.

"Oh, I'm so sorry! How rude of me," she quickly apologized. My name is Shirley."

She extended her hand across the table to shake May's hand. But then May both held up a bloodstained hand and shook her head.

Shirley involuntarily shuddered at the sight of the blood on the other young woman's hands. *Ugh! But really what did I expect?* She glanced behind May at the wide metal tub in which lay several dead carcasses.

"Sorry, babe, can't shake," May said. "You don't want any blood messin' with your pretty manicure."

"Oh . . . of course," Shirley quickly agreed. "Nice to meet you."

"So, Shirley, this is May," April announced. Then focusing her attention on her sister, she asked: "How's mamma doing today?"

May shrugged. "Fair-to-middling. She probably needs another Xanax or two to level her out."

Shirley glanced questioningly at April. She didn't really want to pry, but April had already stated that she'd need to explain about her mother before Shirley met her.

April shrugged too at her inquiring expression. "Mamma's name is Star and sometimes she's in outer space, too. But she means no harm. Pay her no mind when you meet her."

Shirley nodded. *Okay, so their mother is crazy.* Not wishing to give any offence to her new friend(s?), she kept quiet and tried to keep her face neutral.

"So, is your friend going be partying with us later?" May asked.

"Probably not," April replied. "She was just visiting town for the day, but she needs somewhere to stay overnight. I suggested she didn't stay at the motel."

May laughed at that. "Yeah . . . no. Not with that psycho, huh?"

April laughed too. "Yeah. Psycho is right! Bates Motel!"

Both sisters laughed a bit longer, while Shirley, who thought she got the joke, smiled uneasily along with their mirth. But truth be told, Shirley really did feel uneasy. Being here in the woodshed with all its memoirs to animal death, was as a start unsettling enough for a city girl like herself; and now to top that there was the revelation that her hostess' mother wasn't exactly right in the head. And above these worries, Shirley couldn't help feeling that there was something strange about these two young women April and May. The closeness of their ages, the continuity in their names and similarity of their faces already had her suspecting that they were actually twins and also she sensed something unspoken between them—wordless communication that seemed to bode ill for someone, though its subject didn't seem to be herself.

May had stopped laughing and was looking at Shirley again with interest.

April continued her previous explanation. "So . . . I said Miss Shirley could stay here for tonight, and then she's going to ride back into work with me tomorrow."

May nodded. "Un-huh? That right?" She got up from her seat, and walked around from behind the table. She stood very close to Shirley and inhaled deeply. "You smell nice . . ." she said. "A lot better than these dead animals in here."

Shirley smiled uneasily. "Uh . . . thank you."

May laughed and stepped up just a little bit closer, till Shirley got the clear feeling of her personal space being intruded on.

"You look kinda tense," May said. "Would you like me to get you a beer or some weed, to help you unwind?"

Shirley's eyes widened in surprise. "Uh . . . no?"

May positioned her bloodstained hands a few inches above Shirley's shoulders, and mimicked massaging movements. "Well, maybe a relaxing massage instead then?" She giggled. "I might even wash my hands for you! Hey, we could both take a bath!"

Shirley did her best not to cringe at May's increasingly playful (or was it seductive?) behavior. May was undeniably gorgeous, but Shirley had never been into girls. She liked guys, and she had Ted with whom she was very satisfied, thank you. She didn't wish to offend either sister, but being blatantly propositioned in a trapper's woodshed seemed just too surreal.

"I think I'm fine for now," she replied May as coolly as she could. "I'm just tired." While speaking she looked pleadingly at April for her assistance.

April had an amused expression on her face, but still she came to Shirley's rescue.

"Yeah, Miss Shirley had her car towed and don't know where they took it," she said.

Shirley was relieved when May backed off a little bit. Laughing, May said: "Pappy should be able to help her out with that."

April nodded. "That's what I was thinking too."

May turned back to Shirley. And then, leaning in like she was about to kiss her, she said. "You'll really like pappy. Let's hope he likes you, too."

She winked at Shirley close up, about an inch from her face. Shirley stood there stunned by the girl's forwardness.

There was something in May's eyes that was more disturbing that sexual. She had no idea how to respond and just waited with a smile frozen on her face, until May backed off and she felt April tugging her arm.

"Come now, Shirley," April said. "Let's go meet mamma."

CHAPTER 15

As the evening progressed, Ted Jamison grew more and more worried that Shirley hadn't called him.

In his office at the law firm of McNeil, Jamison and Young, he sat at his document-covered desk, talking into his cellphone.

"Hey, babe, it's me again. Give me a call when you get this, huh?"

While he held the phone to his ear with his right hand, his left hand sifted aimlessly through the papers on his desk; picking things up and dropping them again. It was a meaningless gesture, a stirring of ashes as it were; but it reflected his current state of mind.

"I don't know if you can't get a signal, or if your battery is out of juice, or what, but like I said in my previous calls, just give me a call when you can, love."

Ted cut the call and sat back at his desk. He scratched his mustache, ran his hand through his dark hair, and looking mildly concerned. To his mind, at the moment there wasn't really any cause for alarm; the reasons he'd just stated on the phone—no network signal, no battery power—were valid enough, but still . . .

He picked up a paper and began reading it. Then he sighed and looked at his watch. 7:30 pm. *Oh, what the hell is going on with Shirley now?* With no way to satisfactorily answer that question, Ted felt a faint stirring of worry—concern about her wellbeing was impossible to avoid considering how much he loved her—but he managed to convince himself that things were still fine with her.

Dammit! Maybe I should just have told Mass Con Energy to hold on, so we could've made the trip together like she suggested.

Ted tried to read again but after a few futile attempts at concentrating, he wound up tossing the sheets aside. He wiped his forehead with his hand, and picked up his phone again.

Clicking on the name 'Shirley,' he began texting her a message. *Hey, why didn't I think of that before? Even in out-of-the-way places like that, there's times when they can get a signal long enough to pick up a text message.*

CHAPTER 16

The interior of the farmhouse was as cluttered as if occupied by hoarders.

Shirley contained her surprise; she'd only seen residences this full of junk on TV. And in those cases she'd never really taken what she'd seen seriously; when a thing was on TV there was always the possibility that it had been staged for the show.

Not here though. This was the real deal. Junk was piled everywhere she turned to look. There was nothing of real value in the piles of junk; there was just a whole lot of it. Newspapers and boxes were stacked on the floor, with other accumulations of things she recognized and some things that she didn't. For instance, there were sets of dolls on a bookshelf next to something that looked like a part of a car engine— the puzzling metal object was shiny and new, but completely out of place where it had been placed.

The whole place was an untidy mess.

Following April's lead, Shirley navigated her way through the clutter into the living room. Shirley had by now decided to just go with the flow here. There was no longer any doubt in her mind that this was a VERY eccentric family she'd stumbled onto. All she could do now was accept their hospitality and try to get a good night's sleep.

As they stepped into the living room, a female voice called from somewhere in the back of the house. "T-Bird, is that you?"

"No, mamma, it's me," April called back. "I brought company."

The voice spoke again. "Company? Oh, I *love* company."

There was the sound of feet approaching the living room, and then April's mother emerged from the rear of the building.

"Sorry, dearie," she said on seeing them. "I was just arranging some dolls on one of our bookshelves."

More dolls on bookshelves? Shirley did her best to remain composed. She remembered now that April's mother was called Star.

Star was heavy-set woman in her early-to-mid forties with long honey-blonde hair and hazel-colored eyes. She was wearing a bath robe; with some kind of pjs underneath. With a smile on her still-attractive face, she agilely danced around the clutter and walked up to Shirley and her daughter, at the latter of whom she peered with a comical expression of reproach.

"But, sweetheart," she said in a slightly theatrical voice and with overstated accompanying arm gestures, "I wish you would have told me you were bringing someone over. I could have freshened up a bit."

That said, she turned to Shirley and said, "Please accept my apologies for the messy house. I didn't tidy today."

Lady, I don't think you've tidied up for the past ten years, Shirley thought in amusement. But she maintained a straight face and politely replied: "That's fine ma'am. Your daughter has been very kind to me." Staring at Star however, Shirley couldn't help but feel slightly chilled. Despite Star's warm welcome, her eyes held a sort of emptiness that Shirley had rarely encountered. *Oh, that's the Xanax her daughters were talking about. She's probably doped up.*

Star was smiling at Shirley's reply. "Oh, I'm glad to hear that. Please sit down . . . take a load off."

Star was gesturing to a couch while speaking, so Shirley did as she'd said. The indicated couch was relatively less-covered with junk than the living room's other furniture. Shirley cleared some papers off of it and sat.

Star then beckoned to April. "You too, honey," she said. "Please sit down. It's soooo nice to see you socializing for a change."

"Oh, ma . . ." April began saying, like she was embarrassed, but then she shoved aside a few newspapers and sat down next to Shirley, smiling.

Star looked at Shirley: "April is such a bookworm. She spends all day in that stuffy courthouse and don't have too many friends. Well, fact is—she don't have *any* friends."

"Mamma!" April protested.

But her mother ignored her and continued addressing Shirley:

"A loner. That's what people would call her. It's like what you see on the TV news . . . when there's been some mass shooting or somethin'. The neighbors always say the killer was 'a loner. Quiet. Kept themselves to themselves . . .' That's ma girl."

Something in Star's words rang a little too true to Shirley, who shifted uneasily on the couch.

"Oh, quit foolin' around, mamma," April protested again. Then she turned to look at Shirley: "Take no notice, Shirley. She's just playing with you. Me, too."

Shirley nodded and smiled. Well, it was only for one night, right? She could survive their weird behavior for the few remaining hours till daybreak.

"Is it okay. if Shirley stays over, mamma?" April asked.

Star nodded emphatically. "Of course, dear. She can stay for as long as we like."

Mother and daughter now both began giggling. There was something very unsettling about their laughter. Shirley suddenly felt too uneasy to remain here. She stood up, with her eyes scanning the room as if looking for the exit.

"Look," she said nicely, trying hard to keep her nervousness from showing in her voice. "I think this is too much of an imposition on you all. If I can just use your phone, I can call a cab."

Star at first looked surprised by her guest's request, and then her lips expanded into a broad smile.

"Oh, bless your heart, child," she said. "We don't have no phone. No call for it." She giggled. "Haha! Get it?—No call. Sometimes, I just kill myself! Oh, no. You can't call anyone from here. We do some hog-callin' at times. But—no. No phone."

Shirley looked at April for confirmation.

April nodded back. "Mamma's right. No cabs either, way out here."

"Just us and the pigs," Star went on. "I'm afraid we're just simple country folk. Or 'hicks,' as you might call us. I guess you city folk think us rednecks backwards, huh? Bet you think we're . . ."

She pointed to her temple, stabbing it repeatedly with her finger, her eyes bulging, tongue lolling out; pulling a crazy face and adding in an equally loony sounding voice: " 'stooo-pid'?"

Shirley shook her head emphatically. "No. No. Not at all," she protested, while waving her hands in front of her. This statement was of course far from the truth. Shirley now wished she'd turned down April's hospitality altogether, or at least accepted it only as far as letting the young woman drive her over to that bed-bug infested motel run by that Norman-Bates-type character she and her possibly lezzie sister were so disparaging of.

Star stopped making the loony face and laughed: "Oh, bless you and your city-slickin' ways, child. I know you're lyin'."

Shirley shook her head again. "I'm not. I don't think—"

"Oh, but you're welcome to stay," Star interrupted her. "I trust April's judgment. No hard feelins, girl."

She laughed prettily, her mirth almost seeming to peel the years away from her so that for a few moments she seemed more like April's elder sister than mother.

"I was just yankin' your chain," she said, looking into Shirley's eyes with a gaze that confirmed she wasn't exactly right in the head.

April seemed to come to Shirley's aid then. "You taken all your medicine today, mamma?"

Star frowned testily at the question. "Course I have, dear."

But Star winked at Shirley as she said this and Shirley was convinced she was lying—that Star *hadn't* medicated herself today; and that she'd *intentionally* avoided taking her pills. Her unease around this woman now turned to actual fear of her; Star seemed unpredictable in a vague and yet portentous way. Shirley felt as if there was real danger hidden beneath the woman's 'crazy' surface; but then, maybe her weird behavior was simply the visible aspect of her mental illness.

With no escape from either her vague sense of danger or from her current surroundings, Shirley let April lead her back to her seat on the cleared couch amidst the debris and clutter.

Bending over her, April whispered, "Told you she's way out there. Don't pay her any heed."

Shirley was nodding her assent to that, when Star snorted loudly in derision in the background. "Hey, I am *still* sittin' here, you know. I heard ya, girl."

Shirley felt an instant return of the dread she'd been feeling. While smiling sweetly at April and Star she vowed to lock the door of her bedroom tonight. She didn't want either April's sister May to come in to try and 'massage her,' as it were, or April's mother Star to come in and do something crazy to her either.

CHAPTER 17

Out in the woodshed May was concentrating on her work. Her workbench was illuminated by a lantern now, and it shed light on the hanging animal skins, making them look transparent, like they were human skins.

May hummed an eerie tune as she skinned a deer's carcass with a wide-bladed Buck knife, absorbed in her work amongst the gore and slickness.

Then the sound of tires spinning on the dirt track outside and the noise of a car engine pulling up to the farmhouse caught her attention.

Grinning, May sprang up from her workbench and, knife in hand, hurried outside.

A wind-chime of bones rattled in the night air.

CHAPTER 18

Okay, now, disposal of the evidence was the part of hunting that Roger Alfred disliked. Yes, he knew it needed to be done, but . . .

Out in the woods, not too far from where he'd made his two recent kills, Roger was digging a hole. The wind was blowing faintly, and a short distance away through the trees he could hear the sound of passing automobiles.

He strained as he sliced his spade into the hard earth, and then pressed all of his weight down on it, bouncing on the business end of the spade when the ground initially refused to give. No question about it; he found the exertion damn difficult.

Wishing he was younger or in better shape for his age, Roger cursed under his breath.

He finally managed to loosen some soil, and then grunting, he shoveled a spadeful of additional earth onto the small pile that marked the progress of his labors. He stopped, wiped sweat from his brow, and then took a moment to assess how much work still remained to be done, mentally measuring the size and depth of the hole he'd so far dug and reminding himself that it had to be much larger and deeper to avoid its contents being unearthed by the rains, or dug up by the wolves and bears.

Contents indeed! Roger glanced over at the two bulky refuse bags that lay waiting on the nearby grass. Both packages were the size and shape of adult human bodies.

He smirked. *No doubt whatsoever about what both of those contain.*

"Yeah, Maw," Roger grumbled as if his mother was actually there with him. "How come it's always me that does the dirty work? The huntin', the shootin', the killin', an the diggin'."

He laughed at the absurdity of the question, his voice carrying a good distance through the trees. Maw was much too old and infirm— and arthritic—to help him hunt. And there was no way she could help him dig any holes.

Then, realizing he'd better just get on with it before someone chanced along, and besides, that night was falling and he needed to get back to the motel, he shrugged and bent back to work, digging.

"The buryin' the bodies . . . it's so time-consumin'," he grumbled anyway. "I'm a busy man. A businessman. There's a whole lot I got to do."

CHAPTER 19

Inside the old farmhouse, Shirley had just gotten through explaining to April and her mother what she'd come here to Williamson for.

The trio of them sat chatting in the living room with Shirley slowly becoming acclimatized to the clutter everywhere and to the oddness of their company. Occasionally while speaking she tapped the attaché case containing her paperwork she had with her for emphasis.

"Ah," April said when Shirley had gotten through explaining about the land deed and Mass Conn Energy purchase. "So that's why you were poring over all those books."

Shirley nodded. "I just didn't expect it to take that long. It is more complicated than I thought . . . cross-referencing the precise details with the—"

Shirley stopped speaking and looked alarmed as the door burst open. On seeing that it was May at the door, bloodstained knife in hand and grinning, she didn't know whether to feel alarmed or be relieved. *Doesn't anyone in this family act normal?*

"Pappy's home!" May announced in delight.

Shirley only stared at her, but she noticed an instant change in the demeanor of her two female companions. May's sister and her mother both now sat upright, straightening their hair and clothes and smiling expectantly. Clearly the daily return of the family patriarch was quite the event.

May held open the door and heralded her father's entrance with a grand, theatrical flourish of her knife.

April's father walked in with a broad smile on his face. "Hey, hey, hey, womenfolk!" he greeted in a loud and pleasant-sounding voice.

"We got us an extra one today, T-Bird," Star said in a subdued and yet clearly excited voice.

Shirley heard this, but didn't pay much attention. Instead she was staring at the man's clothing: What 'T-Bird' was wearing was clearly a sheriff's uniform. Shirley felt both shocked and confused.

She realized that Sheriff T-Bird was looking curiously at her. The sheriff was a large and quite handsome man and seemed your regulation lawman, but in these family surroundings—boisterous purple-haired daughter, overly conservative daughter, and clinically-crazy-sometimes-Xanax-using wife—there had to be something wrong with him for sure; he was either the creator of the strangeness in his family, or if that wasn't the case, whatever had affected the others was certain to have affected him too.

T-Bird smiled at Shirley. "Well, now, what have we here?"

Shirley stared at April. Understandably, she felt betrayed. And now she was beginning to feel angry; as if she'd been played for a fool.

April, however, was laughing. "Surprise! Shirley—this is pappy. Pappy, this is Shirley."

Shirley shook her head in disbelief: "But . . . all along, you knew . . . Why didn't you say?"

April shrugged. "No point to doin' so. Off-duty since 4 o'clock, like I said, and no way to contact him. He's only Sheriff on the streets . . ."

Star faked a groan of ecstasy. "And my man between the sheets!"

Her daughters both laughed at that. Shirley didn't find the joke funny, and she was relieved to see that T-Bird himself looked both serious and sympathetic.

April seemed to also notice Shirley's dismay. "Aw . . . sorry, Shirley. But I knew he would come home soon, and then all would be well."

April seemed sincere; Shirley wanted to believe that she was. Thinking so helped normalize the current situation a bit.

Sheriff T-Bird said, "Someone want to fill me in on what's happening?"

So, April explained: "Shirley wanted to see the sheriff who towed away her car this afternoon. And here you are."

Shirley looked from father's to daughter's face, trying to assess the situation. Smiles were playing on both April's and T-Bird's lips, but she didn't know what those smiles meant. Were they merely both amused or, was it some kind of unspoken family communication like what she had earlier thought she'd sensed between April and May?

But then T-Bird laughed aloud. And next, as if a sort of ice had been broken by his doing so, everyone laughed, including Shirley, though she laughed only faintly, and while shaking her head as if shaking her bemusement from her mind.

The laughter ebbed after a while and T-Bird stared gravely at Shirley. "So that was *your* car, little lady? In contravention of parking regulations?"

Shirley frowned and tried to sound as apologetic as she could. "I'm sorry, but . . ."

She'd sort-of run out of words. She didn't want to sound like she was begging, because that would make her seem guilty, when she'd acted in innocence and ignorance.

But thankfully April came to her rescue: "Oh, pappy—we're friends, now," the sheriff's serious daughter said. "Can you make an exception? Let the poor girl go get her car?"

Shirley carefully studied the sheriff's facial expression. He seemed to be considering April's request.

"Pretty please, pappy?" April went on.

While twirling her knife between her fingers, May weighed in too: "Chick's cool, pa. Give her a break."

Shirley decided she could beg a little too: "I'm most sincerely sorry, Sheriff," she said. "I'm happy to pay any fine. Any price. I just need my car, please."

T-Bird peered closely at her. "Any fine, huh? You'll pay *any* price?"

Shirley nodded: "Anything." She was relieved that he seemed to be softening towards her. How much could the fine in these parts be? It couldn't be as much as in the city, that was for sure.

But then the Sheriff grinned at her. "Any damn thing, huh?" and she felt uncomfortable again. He wasn't saying or suggesting anything improper; and she didn't think he would do so in front of his family anyway, who appeared to worship the ground he walked on, but she thought she sensed a hint of something creepy about the man now.

Her worries must have reflected on her face, because T-Bird suddenly laughed aloud and smiled reassuringly at her.

"Ah, now, look. No need for that, okay?" He looked at April and May, his gaze flitting from one to the other of them and then broke into a broad grin.

"Never could resist my daughters sweet-talking me," he told Shirley. "Wrapped me round their goddamn fingers."

Then he sighed, shook his head, and looked at his watch: "It's still early. I'm busy later, see. Very busy with important business. We all have jobs to do. Paid or unpaid. As you know, girls."

He grinned at his daughters and they giggled right back. Shirley waited expectantly.

"But well, there's time yet," he went on. Then he looked at Shirley. "All right. Want me to take you round to the impound yard so you can pick up your car?"

Shirley found it impossible to hide her relief. "Now? Oh! Would you? That would be great! Thank you!" She flung looks of gratitude at the two sisters.

Star said, "Unless you'd rather stay the night here? Pick it up tomorrow?"

Shirley shook her head. No way was that ever happening. No way in hell was she sleeping in *this* house. With her luck, any bedroom she got would likely be piled to the rafters with junk also.

But they'd been nice to her, and she really didn't want to be rude to them.

So now she controlled her delight at soon being able to depart from this junk-filled house and its strange occupants, and replied calmly and with gratitude in her voice, "Oh, thank you so much, but no, I mustn't. My fiancé is expecting me back home, and I'm already very late. I haven't even been able to get a phone signal to call him . . . He'll be so worried."

"Ah now, well, that's no good.," the sheriff agreed. "Yeah, cellphone signals don't reach here, as a rule. But we got us a land phone in the office down at the impound yard. You can ring him from the yard. Put his mind at rest."

"Oh, could I?" Shirley said. "That would be such a relief!"

He nodded back with a warm smile. "Course you can, young lady. My pleasure."

Shirley quickly gathered up her purse and package of documents and got to her feet. She felt very relieved now. Once she could put through a call to Ted and let him know she was okay, she'd feel a whole lot better. Hey, she might even decide to spend the night in the bed-bugged motel.

"Well, ladies, I'll be back home in a li'l bit," Sheriff T-Bird told his womenfolk.

"Yeah, don't be long, honey,' Star said, with April and May nodding their heads to that.

"After you, miss," he told Shirley and so they both left the house.

Behind them, April and May exchanged a series of meaningful looks and Star smiled to herself, seemingly lost somewhere in outer space.

CHAPTER 20

As the pair of armed guards patrolled the perimeter of the impound yard they could hear the hubbub of excited voices coming from within the fenced off compound.

The guards smiled at themselves and stared across the junkyard environment, over and between the rows of automobiles and piles of miscellaneous metal objects, at the flaming ring of torchlight in the middle of the yard and an indistinct murmuring sound, a noise which, once one was close enough, became clearly recognizable as the regular chanting sound of many voices.

At particular points, when the lighting was just right, the guards could see those chanting—shadowy figures standing around a clearing within the impound, each figure holding an old-fashioned flaming torch aloft.

Up close to them, the noise is deafening.

CHAPTER 21

"Hey, babe, I'm getting really worried now about not hearing from you," Ted said into his cellphone.

Leaving his desk, Ted stepped to the window of his office and peered out into the dusk. "Hoping you just have no service or whatever," he went on, as he watched the vehicles speed left and right along the road. "Or maybe that you lost your phone, even. Hoping you just needed to find a hotel to stay over for the night. Maybe couldn't get access to the records today, and you'll try again tomorrow?"

He stopped speaking, stepped away from the window again, and wiped his eyes. He felt exhausted; recording into Shirley's voicemail for the umpteenth time tonight wasn't helping his growing anxiety one bit. But he couldn't help himself; couldn't keep from constantly trying her line.

By now Ted was really, really worried. He had a strong feeling that something was very wrong out there in that backwoods county he'd sent her to.

"Hey, just listen to me," he told the phone. "I'm just rambling. Just trying to find reasons why you haven't yet been in touch. But, hey, babe, it's all I can do. I love you, Shirl. Just give me a call when you can, huh, honeybunny?"

He hung up, a stricken look on his face.

CHAPTER 22

Now that her father had driven out again, May was back working in the woodshed under the lamplight.

With her bloody hands she carefully stretched and flayed the final bit of skin off of a rabbit's carcass and then tossed the cold body into a bucket she kept by her left leg for just that purpose.

She took a moment to draw air into her lungs and then yelled: "Mamma! We got us another rabbit ready for the pot here!"

Okay, so maybe she didn't really need to shout so loud, but otherwise sometimes no one heard her.

That statement made, May lifted up the rabbit skin and grinning, her eyes glowing with delight, examined it delicately.

Then, smiling, she added, "And I . . . well I got me a pretty new skin for myself."

CHAPTER 23

The ride to the impound yard was quiet and uneventful; the sheriff said little other than to comment on how dangerous the woods were getting at night nowadays. He explained that people were going missing—the most recent two kids he knew who had gone out just this afternoon for a possible tryst and hadn't been seen since.

Shirley just nodded politely. She wasn't certain what to say and didn't want to get on the sheriff's wrong foot again just when she was about to get her car back.

Not seeming to mind her reticence, Sheriff T-Bird piloted the police cruiser off of the highway that connected to his home and then back onto another dirt road which if anything was even more 'backwoods' than the one that reached his house.

After a first burst of fright that the sheriff was reneging on his earlier promise to take her out to the impound yard and was instead ferrying her off to some remote location to do something wicked to her, Shirley heaved a silent sigh as a chain-link-fenced enclosure suddenly loomed ahead. Behind the wire mesh she could make out the shapes of cars.

Night had fallen completely now and the lights were on.

Although Shirley had never been to an impound yard before, she couldn't help wondering why this isolated place had such a heavy guard presence. As the sheriff drove up to the gate, a wicked-looking man holding a large rifle stepped out of concealment and rolled the iron gate aside.

The sheriff nodded to the man and then drove past him, made a right turn around the internal perimeter of the yard, then made a left turn and drove up an aisle between parked vehicles, so many vehicles in fact that Shirley also began wondering where they all came from, as this impound yard was literally in the middle of nowhere.

The ride through the yard's silent metal tenants was a brief one. At one point during this brief transit however, Shirley thought she heard human voices close by, but the sound vanished a moment later and she realized that she had merely heard one of the guards calling to another one.

Almost immediately afterward, the police cruiser pulled up at the far end of the driveway, almost opposite an office building with its lights off.

The night was silent as death as T-Bird and Shirley got out of the cruiser.

"Thank you so much, sheriff," Shirley said with heartfelt sincerity. "You've saved my life."

T-Bird laughed. "Oh, I wouldn't say that."

Shirley looked around for Ted's BMW. At first glance it didn't seem to be nearby.

"So . . . I don't know," she said. "What do I do now? Do you need me to sign something? I'm happy to pay the fine . . ."

The sheriff shook his head. "Hey, hey, miss! Now, we already went through this. No need for that." He nodded over towards the office building. "There's your car there, beside the pickup truck. Safe and sound."

Shirley now noticed the car. "Oh, goodness. Yes. Thank you," she said.

"You say it's your boyfriend's car?" the sheriff asked with sudden interest.

Shirley nodded. "Yes, my fiancé's. But I am registered to drive it."

Sheriff T-Bird laughed. "Don't worry, girl. Not gonna check your credentials. I have faith. I just thought you said you wanted to let your guy know you're okay." He nodded towards the office building. "Phone's over there, in the office."

"Oh yes, thank you," Shirley said.

They walked over in the direction of the office.

"I really can't thank you enough," Shirley said as they crossed the short space beyond the hood of the BMW.

T-Bird laughed. "Oh, seems like you can."

They both laughed at that and Shirley felt slightly embarrassed.

"Sorry, I do go on," she apologized. "But I am genuinely grateful for everything."

On that statement, Sheriff T-Bird's face squeezed up into a strange expression, and his smile turned a little cold and unpleasant. "Aww. Well, now, if I were you, I would save your thanks."

It was a strange comment for sure, but Shirley felt too elated at her good fortune of finally getting this over with to dwell on it. And besides, by now they had reached the entrance porch leading into the office. The sheriff stepped aside and gestured for Shirley to climb the steps ahead of him.

"Ladies first," he said.

"Oh, thank you."

Shirley stepped up onto the porch but then froze when a large figure suddenly lurched out of the darkness of the office and onto the porch, looming in front of her.

Once over her initial surprise at the figure's appearance, she immediately got another shock. The person standing there was Big Jim, the sleazy gas station attendant.

Too confused to make sense of things, she gasped and stood stock-still.

Big Jim was still his dirty fat leering self. "Well, hello again, sweet cheeks," he said with a look at Shirley that filled her with revulsion. "Come for your Big Jim discount, have ya? Well, I'm ready." He licked his lips so she had no doubt what he was suggesting.

"What the hell . . . ?" Shirley sputtered, turning to stare at the sheriff. To her horror, she saw that Sheriff T-Bird was smiling at her.

"You did say you would pay any price, right?" he asked with a nasty look in his eyes that chilled her in an entirely different way from Big Jim's revolting looks of lust.

And now, she realized that there were others there with them; lots of shadowy figures that now came into view, stepping out into the light, emerging both from within the office, from around the sides of the building, and from behind both her parked car and several others near it.

Male and female, these individuals were all dressed in animal furs and several of them also wore grotesque skeleton headdresses.

Shirley gaped at them in fright and then stared back at Big Jim and T-Bird. "What the fuck is going on?"

"By way of introduction—meet the members of The Clan, girl," Big Jim laughed. "They're sure as hell pleased to meet you."

The Clan? What fucking Clan? Oh, my God, they're a cult! I'm about to be kidnapped by a cult!

Shirley turned to run, but she was already surrounded. She did manage to descend the porch steps, but before she had taken three steps further, the grotesquely garbed people had grabbed her.

"Let me go!" she screamed, but no one paid her the slightest attention. Almost before she'd worked out what was happening, they were both gagging her and tying her up.

She looked desperately over at the sheriff, who nodded calmly back at her.

"Take her away and prepare her!" T-Bird said in a voice of calm authority.

Shirley tried to keep struggling but she was summarily lifted off her feet and borne off across the impound yard by her captors.

CHAPTER 24

A short while after Shirley was seized, the impound yard's lights were suddenly all turned off, throwing the entire compound into darkness.

Now the chanting sound resumed. And this time, as though given fresh impetus by the just successfully concluded abduction, the chanting was louder than before.

Once again, from what had been the pitch darkness that seemingly filled a roughly circular space devoid of cars at the center of the impound yard, flickering flames emerged, light coming from darkness and illuminating scattered and random details—things that were initially blurred and vague, and were indistinguishable from one another.

But as the number of clan members in the space increased and the illumination there thus intensified, a massive metal sculpture was revealed as the thing the cultists congregated before and around.

Lifted high above the heads of the clan members, the violently struggling and terrified Shirley had been carried over to this place and deposited on the ground. And now, from where she had been placed, she stared up at the strange construct in amazement.

If she was already confused by her abduction, this odd structure confused her even more. From where she lay, she couldn't see it clearly, but it seemed to be a pile of scrap metal. A mad structure built from the cast-off parts of cars.

Why are we here? What the hell is this crazy thing? What the hell do these crazy people want with me? They're a cult! What did T-Bird mean when he told them to prepare me!?

These were the questions that flooded Shirley's mind as she lay there helpless, questions that kept repeating and that she would have loved answers to. But they also were questions she found it impossible to concentrate on. Her fear, her anticipation of the horrible things she was certain would shortly follow, made logical thinking almost impossible for her. And the noise, the cultists' chanting filled her with anxiety, expelling logic and replacing it with even more dread and terror.

***

The Clan stood there in reverence, waiting for the most special one of their number. And then she appeared, illumined by the many handheld wavering tongues of fire they held around her.

She stood out clearly from the others. She was statuesque, both alluring and sinister.

At her appearance, the clan swarmed forward around her, and thus obscured her from Shirley's view. But what little Shirley could make out of the new arrival from between the press of fur-clad forms surrounding her was scary enough:

Impossibly, this sexy creature that the cultists were flocking around while ululating to the heavens seemed to be half woman and half a grotesque mixture of animal—maybe wolf and rabbit. Shirley had a momentary glimpse of flesh and fur, and of pale skin and long sharp claws and then the woman-beast was swallowed up again by her followers.

Oh, my dear God, what have I walked into, Shirley wondered in dread.

Then she heard a guttural voice that sounded like a growling bear proclaim: "Prepare her!"

Nooo! she thought. *Noooo!*

But they were already coming for her. She felt faint as many hands grabbed her again and the torment began.

ACT TWO:
TED'S MISFORTUNE

CHAPTER 25

By the next morning, Ted Jamison was in no doubt whatsoever that something was wrong with his fiancée.

Seated at his huge desk, phone pressed to his ear, he frowned in concern while leaving yet another voicemail for Shirley. "Darling? . . . This is, like, the twentieth message I've left on your voicemail."

Ted sighed. He was now at a total loss as to what to do.

Then he noticed Robbie McNeal, one of his partners, peeking in through his office door with some papers in hand. Robbie was clearly hesitating because Ted was on the phone; wondering whether to wait or maybe leave and return later. Ted raised a hand to him and distractedly waved him in. He felt a kind of relief. Robbie's presence would give him something else to talk about.

Robbie, a tall blonde guy in a navy business suit, sauntered in and sat in the chair on the opposite side of Ted's desk.

Ted pinched his left thumb and index finger together in the 'gimme a minute' sign and resumed speaking into his phone: "Look . . . I'm guessing your cell ran out of battery . . . or the car broke down or . . ." It was intensely frustrating. Ted realized that for want of anything else to say, he'd been repeating the same thing in all his voicemails to his missing fiancée.

Robbie was watching him in amusement. Ted ignored him. They were good friends, but he really wasn't in any kind of a clowning mood.

"Hoping you just couldn't call and just found somewhere to stay overnight," Ted said. "I am really worried sick now. Just phone me, soon as you can, huh?"

Robbie was waving the papers at him. He nodded back at him, irritated, and kept addressing himself to the cellphone. "I'm in court this morning, but if I don't hear from you soon—I am coming to find you."

Robbie, mimicking his voice, said: "I will find you. And I will kill you."

Ted glared at him. Robbie made an innocent gesture of holding up his hands. "Not me, buddy—Liam Neeson in *Taken!*"

Ted rolled his eyes and said, "Okay, love ya," into the phone.

Robbie said, "And I love you too."

Ted cut the call and scowled at Robbie. "Fuck you, Robbie."

Robbie grinned back. "I'd only let you do that as an expression of our love, after we're married."

Ted shook his head. "I'm in no mood for jokes, Robbie. Shirley's gone missing."

Robbie still wasn't taking him seriously though: "Hmmm. Maybe she got a better offer?"

Ted stared him down, trying to convey the seriousness of the situation, but Robbie was having his fun and wasn't yet to be dissuaded. "Vicious look, Ted. Practicing for a mugshot? Hey, maybe we should get you a lawyer?"

Ted frowned questioningly. "Huh? You've lost me?"

"Oh, you know: the husband is always the first suspect in any murder investigation."

Ted scowled intently at him: "Not funny, McNeal. Not funny at all."

"Hey, man, she'll be fine, you'll see," Robbie said in a conciliatory voice. "Meanwhile, we've got a trial to go to."

"Yes, don't I know it?" Ted agreed in a disgusted voice. He would much rather remain here in the office and wait for Shirley to get in touch with him, but duty called. They really did have to be in court—he checked his watch—in about twenty minutes.

He snatched up the pile of files he'd prepared for the trial and dashed out of the office, leaving Robbie staring after him in some bemusement.

Figuring Ted couldn't actually leave for court without him in the car, Robbie took his time with getting to his feet.

"Don't wait on my behalf," he mused to himself and then also left Ted's office.

CHAPTER 26

April felt extra good that morning at work. In fact, several of her co-workers wondered while the usually ultra-serious young woman was smiling so much today.

After flinging the door to her office open, April threw her jacket over a chair, dropped her purse on the floor, and sauntered over to the coffeemaker. Once the coffee was brewing, she turned away from it with a broad grin on her face, beaming as if greeting someone arriving to request her help with locating some records.

Someone like that city woman yesterday—Shirley.

"Oh, good morning," April told her imaginary visitor. "And it really *is* a good morning. Today's a glorious day, isn't it?"

She wasn't too worried about someone coming in and finding her talking to herself; she had few friends here. Besides, visitors with inquiries about old records normally didn't start arriving until about ten or eleven a.m.

She laughed, remembering another beautiful sunny day just like this one, with the birds singing in the trees while a cool breeze gently moved the leaves about; herself and May standing in the shade, watching the sunlight spill onto the forest floor in shifting dappled patterns that mimicked the swaying leaves on the branches overhead.

"In fact, this is the kind of day that makes you feel happy to be alive." April said in amusement as she walked back to the coffeemaker to pour out her coffee.

This wasn't an idle statement. That other beautiful and sunny day she had just been remembering had been significant for another reason too. Even now, picture-perfect in her mind, she could visualize the grave beside the trees—it had been a man-sized area of exposed soil, stamped down and sketchily scattered over with leaves and grasses in a half-hearted attempt to disguise it against the rest of the ground.

As April poured her coffee, she reflected on how nice digging that grave had been. Truly the kind of experience worth repeating.

CHAPTER 27

Shirley's prison was a dark and windowless shed, with slits of sunlight showing in the gaps between the planks that comprised the walls and illuminating the darkness within. It was a wooden compartment within the boundaries of the impound yard—a cell built of timber planks, a tin roof, and an earth floor.

Shirley lay face-down on the ground, her limbs loose as if she had been thrown there; which was an accurate description of how she'd arrived at that position on the floor. Her previously immaculate clothes were dirty and torn, her erstwhile clean face and arms bloodied, her just-recently styled hair a shapeless and tangled mess.

Shirley groaned.

Slowly, she began moving, her consciousness returning. Once she was awake enough to recall her current straits, she eased herself up into a sitting position on the ground, all the while wincing with pain.

As if drugged, she gazed around dully, her eyes quickly taking in the dimensions and particulars of her prison; the few contents amidst its general lack of furniture.

Oh, my God no! she thought as a bolt of terror surged up through her and she fought to suppress it. *What in the world have I stumbled onto here? These people . . . the sheriff . . . Big Jim . . . they're crazy . . . crazy*

But she had already—unsuccessfully, without reaching any satisfactory answers—run through the gamut of questions and emotions last night. Now she stopped pondering and considered the state of her body.

She hurt both inside and outside.

Her wrists were raw, stinging from deep rope burns. She tentatively licked the angry bruises, emitting small hisses of hurt when their pain flared up.

She recalled exactly what the cultists' so-called 'preparation' had consisted of. Beatings and sexual defilement, that was what. It had been a degrading and nauseating experience; something she hardly dared to let herself remember. The strange half-beast, half-woman creature she had glimpsed almost seemed an illusion to her now. By the time she'd been stripped naked and her violation begun, the woman-thing had vanished again; and all that was left were her own terrors.

So maybe, the woman-beast was part of her night terrors too—a figment of her imagination.

Wincing in pain, Shirley rose to her feet, testing her legs, which felt like jello. Each step she took had her feeling as if she instantly crumble down into a pile of human jelly, but she got herself moving. This wasn't any sort of time to grant her aches and bruises priority—no matter however serious they were.

So, forcing herself to remain upright, Shirley slowly and tentatively explored her prison. It was bleak, there was nothing to either see or explore in here, as the shed contained no furniture whatsoever; it just had two wooden support pillars in its middle that rose through the ceiling. Seeing as it had no windows either, she tried to peer through the vertical gaps between its timbers, while her fingers put pressure on its walls, testing them for any weakness. She was careful not to bang on the walls, she didn't want to alert any guards outside that she was trying to get out. Her dirty fingers picked at the gap around the door; searching for looseness, for a space she could exploit.

Her search was however in vain. This might be a makeshift wooden cell, but it was a sturdy and a secure one.

One thing she did notice however, though the knowledge was useless to her, was the pig pen a short distance away, between this shed and the impound wall. The pigs were mostly silent, as if sleeping, but their smell was only slightly less potent than that which she'd encountered on her ride to April's farmhouse.

Once Shirley had established that for the moment, she had no way out of here, she leaned against a sturdy upright timber and did some thinking. She had no idea if there was cellphone reception here in the impound yard, but the knowledge would be a moot point anyway—along with the documents she'd brought to town, her purse and phone had been taken away from her.

The county sheriff and his family were members of an insane cult Last night, Shirley had gotten a taste of just how depraved the cult was, and there had been hints of worse to come, hints of additional gruesome and unwholesome activities.

Her terror returned and once more she forced it away. She knew she mustn't panic.

There has to be a way out of here.

She'd been both beaten and sexually abused; Big Jim in particular had made good on his promise to give her his 'Big Jim discount.' Thankfully Shirley's mind was currently blanking out the full extent of the sexual torment she had suffered at the cultists' hands; if she remembered exactly what these deranged people had done to her she might snap for good. What she currently recalled of her ordeal was that it had seemed endless, and that both men and women had abused her.

And afterwards she had been thrown in here.

This shed was part of the impound yard, on the opposite side from the front gate. After being borne down an aisle of cars, she had been unceremoniously dumped in here and untied. Then, her fur-and-bone-clad captors had returned back the way they'd come. Through a crack between the planks, she'd watched the departing flames of their torches melt away between the rows of cars, back towards the center of the yard.

Shirley began feeling a long overdue call of nature.

She grimaced at the pair of buckets that had clearly been placed against one of the walls for this eventuality. One bucket was filthy and empty and had a roll of toilet paper next to it; the other bucket was full of clear water.

Intense pain shot through Shirley's body as she knelt beside the water bucket and cupped her hands, scooping water thirstily into her mouth and drinking deeply.

Then she rubbed the water across her face, smearing blood and dirt with the water while she attempted to clean herself.

Next, after regarding the other, soiled bucket with disgust for a while and pondering her options and realizing it was either use the bucket or do her business on the dirt floor, she unraveled some toilet paper; and crouched over the pail, urinating loudly. The patter of her water against the bottom of the metal bucket felt unnecessarily noisy. She cried out with pain and wept.

Once through peeing, Shirley wiped herself clean with a wad of toilet paper. Knowing what she was about to see, she tried not to look at the toilet paper when she was done using it. But she had nowhere else to discard it other than inside the bucket, and while doing so she couldn't help seeing the flimsy tissue's soaking of blood and blood clots.

The obscene sight brought back the memory of last night's sexual abuse; a sliver of memory managed to sneak through the psychic barrier her mind had erected to keep it away from her, and when Shirley recalled even that little portion of what they had done to her, she felt like she was loosing her mind and she began weeping.

With her eyes full of tears, Shirley eased herself into a corner of the room, and sat there hugging herself, making herself as small as possible; as small as she currently felt.

To comfort herself, she told herself that Ted was certain to have begun searching for her now.

In fact, I'm certain that by now he must be worried stiff about me!

CHAPTER 28

Shirley was one hundred percent correct in her assumption and hope that by now Ted would be searching for her.

Her fiancée and his two legal partners were just arriving back from the court.

With both Robbie McNeal and their other partner Stan Young hot on his heels, Ted rushed back inside his office.

Robbie looked very perplexed. "Dude, you applied for the trial to be pushed back because your girlfriend won't answer your calls?"

Ted scowled at him. Yes, Robbie was one of his closest friends since college—they went way back—but sometimes the guy just acted so fucking obtuse. He wondered what it would take for Robbie to think there was a crisis—another 911 or a nuclear war?

"That's fiancée, not girlfriend—fiancée means there's an additional layer of seriousness and commitment. And no, I didn't push back the trial date because I can't find Shirley. . . . *We three* got the date put back because we need time to process extra evidence—that the judge agreed to give us time to collect . . ."

Stan, a plump good-natured man who seemed out of calling as a lawyer, grinned at Robbie. "Never accuse Ted of being remiss in his professional conduct, Robbie."

"But yes, if you must know," Ted went on, "I am also concerned because Shirley has gone missing and I need to find her."

Robbie still looked amused. Stan had sat in one of the client's chairs in the office, and Robbie perked himself on the edge of Ted's desk. Ted, whose office it was, wasn't sitting down. He hovered over his desk like a hawk looking for prey, with his eyes revealing his agitation. Ted hadn't even put down his legal files yet, and he still had his jacket slung over his forearm. He looked from one friend's face to the other as if seeking answers in their eyes.

"Hey, isn't this a bit of an overreaction?" Robbie asked.

Stan looked at him severely. "Lay off, Robbie. This is getting serious. If you can't help or say something supportive, say nothing."

Robbie at first looked like he'd make an amusing retort to that, but then his face turned somber too. "Okay. So . . . maybe she had an accident? Have you tried calling anyone? Hospitals?"

Ted nodded. "I called the West Virginia State Police late last night. They had been advised of no road accidents. And they said they won't do anything to help till she's been missing for at least forty-eight hours. They say she's not a vulnerable person." He kicked the leg of his chair, causing it to shift abruptly to the side and making both Robbie and Stan gape at him in surprise. "But . . . dammit!"

Ted finally seemed to realize that he was still carrying the legal files he'd taken to court. In exasperation, he flung them down on his desk. Then, after a brief look around (in which he hardly appeared to notice his two companions) he picked up a briefcase standing beside the office wall, opened it up on the desk and began flinging things into it.

"Shirley can take care of herself, Ted," Robbie said. "I mean, she can be ballsy when she's riled. I know from experience. *I* wouldn't mess with her."

Stan nodded. He agreed with Robbie that Shirley wasn't a pushover, but he could also see that Ted was above listening to exhortations of Shirley's competence to deal with whatever situation she'd found herself in.

"You got GPS," he said. "Use your BMW Assist feature to try to locate the car."

Ted shook his head. "You can only do that if the vehicle is stolen. I'm sure that's not the case here."

Robbie said, "Shoot down every idea, why don't you? We're just trying to help you out."

Stan frowned. "Robbie! Can't you see he's distressed? Have some fellow feeling. Thank God you didn't go into family law. You'd have goddamned bankrupted us by now. Ted, look—if there's anything we can do . . ."

Ted stared at him with a mixture of gratitude and worry. "I'm just worried that she might be in danger, or sick . . . or maybe had some kind of accident that the police don't know about."

Stan nodded. "Look, you do what you've got to do, Ted."

"I should go try to find her myself, Stan. I can't rest," was Ted's desperate reply, after which he picked up his briefcase and jacket, and made as if to leave the office.

"Sure," Stan said encouragingly. "We'll hold the fort here and cover for you."

Ted headed for the door, then turned back and nodded solemnly at both men.

Robbie opened his mouth as if to say something suitably humorous to lighten Ted's dire mood, but Stan shot a warning look at him, and so all he said instead was, "Honestly, Ted—don't worry. I am sure Shirley's fine!

Ted nodded and then was out the door, leaving Robbie and Stan staring at each other.

CHAPTER 29

Roger sat behind the motel's reception desk, all smiling hospitality. His thoughts however, if they were exposed to the light of day, would have caused any prospective clients of his huge alarm:

Oh yes, indeed. The hunting here IS good. This is definitely an area for shooting. Trapping. Whatever you like. Yup. We have a variety of critters. Squirrels . . . groundhogs. But that's child's play. Boars . . . deer . . . bears, yes. Oh, and of course, it's always open season for tourists.

He grinned with delight to himself: *No, folks, I mean, for those of us who hunt down tourists.*

Roger laughed and resumed mentally addressing his nonexistent audience. *Only joking, people. Just a little West Virginian joke. An Appalachian jape. Funny, huh? We have to make our own entertainment out here. Otherwise a person would go mad, wouldn't they? Stark staring bat-shit crazy. So, I like a joke, now and again. I think we all do, don't we? I know my mother does.*

Roger settled down to wait for some tourists. They seemed in rather short supply nowadays; almost like someone really had been killing them off. No joke.

CHAPTER 30

It was a long drive down across the southern state line, and then through the increasingly backwards countryside, but by early evening Ted had arrived in Ringo County.

With his car in Shirley's possession, he'd been forced to drive her own car, an old Toyota Camry. He considered this turnaround very ironic—seeing as the reason Shirley had left her car behind in the first place was because she'd figured it wouldn't survive the trip here. But the old jalopy had handled admirably, not that Ted would trust it on any regular basis either.

Alright, now here seems a good enough place to start my enquiries, he thought on spotting the BIG JIM'S GAS UP fuel station up ahead.

He'd still heard nothing from Shirley since setting out from Pittsburgh, which was clearly a confirmation that something had gone very wrong on her trip. But now he had the satisfaction of being on her trail. Yes, he'd so far discovered nothing, but now that he was here, it shouldn't be too hard to start an investigation into her disappearance.

Hey, stop jumping the gun and assuming the worst! Implausible as it seems at the moment, there's probably a very logical explanation for this.

He turned off the road into the gas station and parked up beside the convenience store. Except for a green pickup truck that was pulling out as he pulled in, the place seemed otherwise deserted.

Ted, who was still wearing his business suit, got out of the car and strode over to the convenience store. After a cursory look around and making a brief mental note of how backwards this place was—like something out of the thirties—he pushed the glass door open and stepped through.

This guy has to be Big Jim, Ted decided with a lawyer's practiced eye on sighting the man sitting behind the cash register. He estimated 'Big

Jim' to weigh about three hundred pounds. He was a large and bald middle-aged chunk of man clad in dirty overalls; unpleasant-looking for sure.

Scratching in his bushy beard with a hand while chewing tobacco, the fat man stared moodily as Ted approached him, clearly assessing his expensive clothes and trying to reconcile them with the not-so-expensive car he could see parked outside the store.

"Evening." Ted nodded to 'Big Jim' who in turn acknowledged Ted with a raise of his quite-bushy eyebrows.

"You jus' pump it yerself, then come pay," he informed Ted with a wave of his hands towards the pump.

Ted hid his adverse reaction to the sight of Big Jim's grimy and untrimmed fingernails. "I don't need gas. Thanks."

Big Jim looked surprised for a few seconds. "Okay. But this is a gas station, 'case you never noticed. So—what can I do for you, man?"

Ted ignored the insult. He refrained himself from in turn pointing out that this was supposedly a convenience store, though it looked like no one ever bought anything in here because of how filthy and unkempt it was.

"I'm looking for someone," he explained.

Big Jim nodded. "Always someone lookin' for someone."

Then to Ted's surprise he spat out a jet of brown tobacco juice directly onto the floor beside him. Ted decided he didn't want to see what the ground behind the counter looked like; the floor on this side of it looked messy enough. In places it was splattered with oddly shaped and colored blobs that nauseatingly reminded him of phlegm.

Big Jim was wiping his lips dry with the back of his hand while staring at Ted inquisitively, so Ted got Shirley's photo out of his wallet and handed it over the counter.

"My fiancée," he explained while doing so. "Have you seen her? She would have passed through here yesterday—maybe lunchtime, maybe early afternoon."

Ted wasn't sure why he did so, but he watched Big Jim closely for any sign of recognition. But Big Jim just glanced at the photo and shrugged. After scanning the photo closely for a few seconds, he looked back up at Ted and shook his head slowly.

"You might remember her car," Ted pressed. "Black BMW?"

But Big Jim stared blankly back at him. "Nope. Think I'da remembered that." Then he smiled, revealing an expanse of discolored teeth. "And your 'fi-an-cee'—she's real purty, I'da def'nitely remembered her."

Ted gave him an uncertain look. Big Jim hadn't said anything out of order by complimenting Shirley's beauty, but still Ted thought he'd detected something in his voice. As an attorney, he was used to people lying to him, suspects and cons trying to pull the wool over his eyes while being cross-examined.

Nah, I'm just being suspicious here, he thought as Big Jim handed the photo back to him. Still, he stared directly into Big Jim's eyes, trying to read them, attempting to see behind their flat gray glare and unearth any dirty secrets buried in their sockets.

Big Jim stared back with a bored look, slowly chewing his wad of tobacco, and looking like he was getting ready to spit again. The sun coming in through the store windows reflected off his head, making the drops of sweat on it stand out.

Ted gave up. "Okay . . . Well, thanks for your help."

Big Jim nodded and Ted turned and left the convenience store. Just in time apparently, because as the store door swung shut behind him, he heard the man expel another gob of spit and also heard the repulsive splat of something wet landing on the floor.

He walked quickly to his car, unaware that Big Jim was staring hard at him all the way.

CHAPTER 31

Shirley knelt near the wooden wall of the shed she was imprisoned in, staring intently at the ground. For about twenty minutes she had been scratching at the surface of the compacted earth floor with her bare fingernails, digging a hole near one of the plank wall posts. The hole was a small one, so far nothing to write home about. She pulled at the plank closest to her hole, but it gave only slightly.

"Son-of-a-bitch!" Shirley grumbled. Her plan still had a way to go then. It was a simple plan. A large enough hole might let her lever several of the planks free and thus create a hole she could slip through. And then escape was merely a question of running to the chain-link fence that ringed the impound yard, which she saw vaguely (just a tantalizing short distance away) whenever she peered through the spaces between the planks.

Her neighbors the pigs were awake now; she heard their squealing.

She resumed digging the hole, ruining her manicure in the process but not in the least concerned about that fact. However, all of her labor was making only a small addition to her hole, and after awhile she sighed in frustration.

"This isn't fucking working. This isn't working at all; I need a tool to dig with," Shirley softly acknowledged to herself.

She got to her feet and looked around, her eyes quickly scanning the shed for anything she could press into service to help her penetrate the hard floor more quickly. And a tool of some kind was important because she wasn't merely weak from the physical abuse that she'd suffered; she'd also not had anything to eat since yesterday, and hunger had begun telling on her body.

Not immediately seeing anything that might help her covert excavation of the shed floor, Shirley bent down again and with her hands began spreading the small heap of earth she had so far scooped out across the floor of the shed, distributing it evenly.

She got this done not a moment too soon, because next she heard a jangling of keys and chains outside the shed. The sound stopped her in her tracks.

Then she quickly placed the water bucket on top of the small hole she had excavated, and next flung herself back against the wall. The water in the bucket sloshed about but quickly settled.

Shirley heard the sound of a heavy bolt being drawn back. And then the door creaked open, light filled the shed, and a large black shadow fell in front of her, cast on the floor by the person standing in the doorway, someone who was still out of view.

Shirley's eyes widened in fear as she anticipated the entry of the still unseen figure.

CHAPTER 32

Ted felt frustrated. One thing that he'd definitely not anticipated on arriving in the little town of Williamson, county seat of Ringo County, was to find the courthouse closed.

But it was closed. Ted had already tried to open the building's front door, pushing and rattling the doorknob, but had finally conceded the fact that the place was locked up.

Slightly perplexed, he looked around, first of all back out into the road, which was mostly deserted, and then back at the building he'd come to. It was only now that he noticed the sign on the wall, to the right side of the door:

'Ringo County Courthouse & Sheriff's Office.
Open: Mondays to Fridays 10 am – 4 pm'

Ted looked at his watch. "Fuck," he said on realizing that he'd arrived in town an hour too late.

Still there was always the chance of stragglers still being in the building; like someone who had work to catch up on or perhaps a janitor, so he hammered on the door with the edge of his fist and yelled: "Hey! Anyone?"

At any other time, Ted would have felt self-conscious at this outburst, but in addition to the desperation he now felt creeping up on him, there was really no one else around to notice his display of raw emotion.

He gave one last hopeless bash to the courthouse door, and then looked up and down the street again. Now he felt there was something creepy in the street's emptiness. Of course, he knew this was dumb, everyone had simply gone home after the day's work.

Well, maybe not everyone. Ted was staring down the road, at the tavern in the near distance. He considered that the local bar might be a good place in which to make some inquiries.

He got out his cellphone to call Robbie and Stan back at the office and let them know he'd arrived okay in Williamson, and then groaned at its 'No Signal' message. The area's lack of cellphone coverage was something that had become apparent shortly after he'd left Big Jim's gas station. Now he partly understood why Shirley hadn't yet gotten in touch with him.

But the understanding didn't bring much relief with it, because the question still remained: *where was she?* Ted knew she didn't need two whole days to check up on what he'd requested that she do, and there was no chance at all that they'd passed each other on the highway; no chance that he'd not recognize his own car if Shirley had been driving it back to Pittsburgh.

And there was another bothersome question: *Why didn't she simply call me from a landline?*

Ted scowled at the cellphone. "Goddamn godforsaken backwoods hick town!"

He put his phone away in his pocket, and after a glance at his car and deciding there was no point driving it such a short distance down the street, set off on foot for the tavern.

As he walked, he pondered on that obvious and now increasingly disturbing question: *Yes, so Shirley's cellphone clearly isn't working here in hick village, but why didn't she call me from a landline? There has to be a number of them here that are working.*

Was it that Shirley hadn't been able to find a serviceable landline, or was she being prevented from using one?

CHAPTER 33

Ted pushed through the tavern door. The interior of the place was dark, with a couple of locals sitting drinking and others playing pool. The bartender looked bored; he sat watching a sports program on a portable TV.

Once properly inside the tavern, Ted instantly became aware that a hush had fallen over the place. Everyone had suddenly gone silent; all eyes seemed to be watching him as he walked over to the bar.

Ted didn't let this bother him; this was a small town and his clothes clearly marked him as an outsider. Oddly, even the TV had gone quiet.

The bartender eyed Ted warily. Maybe he thought Ted was here to enquire about unpaid back taxes or something like that.

Ted smiled at him. "Can I get a beer, please?"

Still silent, the bartender poured him a beer.

Ted pulled Shirley's photograph from his pocket and flashed it at the bartender. "I'm looking for this lady. She would have arrived in town yesterday? Seen her around?"

The bartender studied the picture for a moment, then shook his head, and gave Ted his beer. Ted began wondering if the man was simply naturally uncommunicative or if maybe he couldn't talk. But no, that couldn't be it; the man had to be able to talk; how else could he run a bar?

More backwoods syndrome to deal with, he thought. But now that he'd bought a beer the initial interest most of the bar patrons had shown in him had waned and they'd gone back to their drinks and desultory discussions.

"Or the sheriff maybe?" Ted pressed on. "I'd like to talk to the sheriff, but there's nobody there—the courthouse is locked."

The bartender nodded and finally spoke: "Yup."

Their conversation so far struck Ted a lot like cross-examining an uncommunicative witness in court. "Just how does this town operate, if you can't get a hold of the sheriff? Crime not an issue here?"

"Not much." The man picked up a washed glass and began wiping it clean.

Ted sipped his drink, wondering exactly how to proceed. The bartender really did seem a naturally taciturn fellow. He glanced around the tavern, wondering if maybe he should show Shirley's picture to the other patrons. As his eyes flickered down the length of the bar he noticed a very attractive young woman with purple hair regarding him over the rim of her glass while she sipped her beer.

There was something in her eyes that seemed inviting, almost like she could be a prostitute, and so Ted quickly looked away from her and back at the bartender.

"You serve any food here?" he asked.

The bartender nodded over at a tattered sign that read: 'BBQ wings – $5'.

Ted, who was becoming used to the man's uncommunicative nature, nodded back at him. "O.K., I'll take some wings too then, please."

After he'd placed his order he became aware of a movement down at the far end of the bar. He watched the purple-haired girl slip off of her bar stool, pick up her beer, and slink over towards him.

Oops, here comes trouble, he thought.

The approaching young woman was indisputably gorgeous. Early-to-mid twenties in age and dressed sexily—tight denim pants and clinging halter top—smoking hot and ready to flirt. She'd obviously taken an interest in him.

"Hey, there, new boy in town!" she greeted.

Ted turned and smiled politely at her and then quickly returned his attention to his drink.

"I apologize," she said in softly coy tones. "I meant 'man,' not 'boy.' Obviously, you're all man. Anyone can see that."

That said, Ted had no choice but to look at her again. Anything else might be considered rude and he had to remember that he was an outsider here.

She was eyeing him and grinning. She extended her hand.

"Hello, I'm May."

They shook hands, but Ted was barely noticing her. Her presence at his side had actually reminded him of why he was here in her town.

However, he discovered that May with the purple hair wasn't to be dissuaded that easily.

Still smiling, she asked: "And *your* name is?"

"Hi, May, I'm Ted." A glance around the tavern showed no one was paying them the slightest interest. Even the bartender was busy preparing the wings Ted had ordered. They could have been old friends, lovers even, for all anyone else in here seemed to care.

"Happy to make your acquaintance, Ted," May said, climbing up on the bar stool next to him. "Mind if I join you?" she asked.

"Um . . . Okay.," Ted said. He resigned himself to having this conversation with her.

She sipped her beer, looked around, and sighed.

"This town is so dull," she said. "Same folks every day. People I grew up with. There's nothing more to say to them. But I sure do love talking to new people."

Ted nodded understandingly. "I'm sorry, but I don't know that I'm exactly good company tonight."

May shook her head. "I'm sure you are!"

Ted smiled sadly. "I'd like to believe that ordinarily I am, but I'm afraid I'm a bit distracted today."

May gave him a look of concern. "I'm sorry to hear that. Can I be of any assistance?"

Ted sighed. "I dunno. See, I'm looking for somebody."

May laughed and shook herself suggestively. "Will *this* body do for you? Well, here I am!"

Oh, lady, you most definitely are here! Ted thought. But he pointedly ignored her comment and passed her the photo of Shirley he'd just shown the bartender.

"Have you seen her?" he asked.

He waited expectantly while May took the picture from him and studied it closely. Finally though, she shook her head. "Can't say that I have. No. Sorry. Can't help you out there, Ted."

Ted nodded. The bartender placed a plateful of wings in front of him.

May giggled at the food. "Could help you out with those, though."

"Go ahead," Ted said, sliding the plate towards her.

"How about we take these wings and fly?" May asked, gazing at him, meaningfully. He pretended not to hear this, wondering if maybe Shirley actually somehow drove to the wrong town.

May persisted, "Hey, want to go somewhere more comfortable?"

Ted decided Shirley wasn't so airhead as to visit the wrong town. "Okay," he agreed and then gestured across the room—"There's a free table over there." He picked up the plate of wings and after nodding at his beautiful companion, led the way over to a dining table with padded seating placed around it.

He didn't notice May rolling her eyes before following him.

"So, what do you do for a living, Ted?" she asked as they walked over to the table.

"I'm a lawyer."

"Hey, I'm impressed!" May said.

Ted noted that she sounded sincere too.

They settled into the seats. Ted placed the photo on the table between them. They started eating the wings.

Chicken wing clamped between her teeth, May asked: So, is that what brings you out here? Looking for this girl? She a criminal? A witness? Who is this?"

While speaking, she tapped Shirley's photo with a finger. Ted winced on seeing her finger leave a stain of BBQ sauce on Shirley's face. He quickly wiped the sauce off with a paper napkin and then replaced the photo in his wallet.

"She's my fiancée, Shirley," he explained to the girl seated opposite him. "She should have arrived here yesterday, but I haven't heard from her for over twenty-four hours."

May shrugged and snapped the bones of a chicken wing apart. "You two have a fight or somethin'?"

Ted shook his head vigorously. "No. No. Quite the opposite . . ."

May shrugged again. "Aw. Maybe she just wants some time to herself. A little fun before her life sentence, married to you. A last fling for Mrs. Ted. We all need a little fun, Ted."

She bit hungrily into a wing and then licked her lips.

"Shirley's not like that," Ted insisted.

"Oh, I'm sure she's okay, Ted. I can feel it. I know these things, 'cause I'm kinda psychic that way. Just call me 'Mystic May'. "

Ted gave her a dubious look. "Well, I hope you're right."

May nodded. "Mmm-hmm . . ." She licked her fingers seductively while staring into his eyes. "Hey, I know. Let's cheer you up." Ted watched her take out her cellphone and then get up and come around to his side of the table. "Hey, let's take a selfie!"

Before he could protest against it, she had squeezed her face against his and was holding out the phone in front of them.

Ted sighed. He was beginning to suspect that this young women who'd latched onto him wasn't exactly right in the head. He looked over at the bartender for help dealing with her, but the bartender was pouring a drink for a couple who'd just walked in and wasn't looking his way at all.

"I'm really not in the mood, May," Ted protested.

"Ah, c'mon," she however insisted. "Make my boyfriend jealous. Look like you're enjoying yourself and smile."

To humor her and get her off of his back, Ted did indeed smile at the camera.

The camera flashed at both of them, but May didn't let him pull away from her yet. "One more!" she insisted brightly. "Hey, hey—keep looking happy!" She kissed his cheek, and her camera flashed again. "See! Smile and you automatically feel happier."

Ted smiled to humor her, but then she squeezed his thigh, and he found himself looking into her eyes, uncomfortably close to her beautiful face and body. Aware of her eyes on him, he cleared his throat and pulled away from her, then quickly reached for another chicken wing and began devouring it.

She grinned at him: "Looks like you're hungering for something, Ted. Hey— what say we go back to this little motel I know on Route 52? It's just down the road a ways, about seven miles out of town."

Ted shook his head: "Oh, I'm very flattered, but I don't think so."

"It's an okay place," May said. "You're safe. It might be the only place to stay for miles around, but they are truly discreet there. No one will know."

"It's not that . . ." *Okay, so here it is out in the open. I was right—she is a prostitute trying to hustle up a little business.*

"I can see you have quite an appetite," May whispered to him. "I like that in a man. And I promise you—I will help you to forget all your woman troubles."

"That's a lovely idea, May, and you certainly are a very beautiful, sexy woman . . . but thank you. No. I'm not really looking for your kind of business tonight. Or any night."

Her reaction surprised him. "Ted! I'm quite insulted . . ." she said, with her eyes only partly amused.

"I don't mean to insult you. Honestly. We all have to make a living."

May gaped at him. "You think I'm a whore? Good religious girl like me? I'm just tryin' to be friendly here. You look like you need some comfortin'. Truth to tell, I'm a little lonely and bored myself. Thought we could both do one another a favor."

Ted sighed; this was becoming complicated. "I do apologize. But I am practically a married man. Also, I love Shirley too much. Sorry, but I just want to find her. I'm worried about her."

"I'm only trying to take your mind off her for a while. Give you a little . . . relief."

By now Ted was very tired of his lovely companion, but he did his best to conceal his irritation. "The way I feel right now, I would be a sad disappointment to you, May. Even if I did take you up on your kind and generous offer."

"Oh, Ted—you would be no disappointment, I'm certain. And rest assured, I know a few tricks that would help you to forget everything. Believe me, I'll blow"—he winced as she pursed her lips at him—"your mind."

He shook his head emphatically. "I am both honored and flattered, May. A eunuch would be turned on by you, I'm sure. But I'm still sorry to say—I will have to say no. I thank you so much, and wish you well. Goodbye."

He could see the anger forming in her face like clouds covering a previously clear sky, but before she could make some acid reply to him, he stood up and picked up his beer, nodded to her, and then headed over to the bar counter.

Behind him, he heard her say in a soft voice: "Fuck you! Well, I literally would have, given half a chance. Loser!"

He was facing partially towards the entrance of the tavern and next witnessed May suddenly storm past him and hurry out through the door, with her face set in fury.

Relieved that she wasn't about making a scene, Ted signaled the bartender.

"Check, please," he told the man. He spent the wait for the check draining the last of the beer from his glass.

The check came. Ted looked at the total, and then got out his wallet from his jacket and passed over a few bills to the barkeep.

Ted raised a finger to hold the man's attention. "Hey, is there anywhere else to stay around here? I hear there's a motel or something on Route 52? Anyplace else?"

The bartender immediately shook his head. "Nope. Not for a good forty-five miles, at least. The Respite Motel over on Route 52 is the only place. Rough and basic, but close enough."

Ted considered this reply for a few seconds, surprised that the previously uncommunicative man had actually strung together that many sentences to reply him, then asked him another question: "And the courthouse opens tomorrow at ten?"

The bartender nodded. "Yes, sir."

Ted nodded back. "Sounds like I have no choice then, if I want to speak to the sheriff?"

"No, sir," the man replied.

Ted nodded again. "Hmm. Thanks. By the way, can you give me directions, please?"

CHAPTER 34

Working amidst the shadows in the scant moonlight that pervaded the shed she was imprisoned in, Shirley was once more digging her proposed bolt hole.

At the moment, she was crouched down low over it and scraping away, her eyes occasionally glinting in the traces of external light that filtered into the shed. Unable to find any real tools, Shirley had taken to using a bent nail to loosen the earth—the nail was in no way optimum, but it reduced the hurt to her hands.

Suddenly she heard the sound of approaching footsteps and voices.

Once more she hurriedly placed the bucket over the hole, and then quickly stepped away from it.

The last time the cultists had come to her—earlier today when she'd just begun digging—they'd brought her some food; a pork sandwich. The food had been extremely welcome. It had strengthened her, allowed her to continue digging.

But only two people came here then, she thought worriedly. *What do so many of them want with me now?*

She suspected that whatever it was, would be very bad indeed. She hoped she wasn't in for another time of sexual abuse. Dread of being once more used as the Clan's perverted sex toy filled her.

The door creaked open then. Light flooded in.

"Well, miss, you'll be a comin' with us now," Big Jim's voice said. "And you'd better come quietly or else . . ."

CHAPTER 35

After leaving the tavern, Ted didn't drive directly to the motel.

He first spent some more time in town, asking around to see if anyone had seen Shirley. When, almost two hours later this line of inquiry had still yielded no results and the sky had begun darkening, he decided he'd best call it a day and go find the motel and get some rest.

Following the bartender's directions, Ted found it easy enough to locate the Respite Motor Lodge on Route 52. The sky was dark by the time he arrived there, night had stolen over the area unawares during his short drive over.

And now, here he was …

Ted sat in the car for a while, regarding the flashing neon 'vacancy' sign. The motel buildings all looked old.

During this sitting interval, he tried to get his worries under control. *I've made some progress, that's the thing. I'm in town and asking questions, and come morning, it's certain that I'll be seeing the sheriff. Once proper inquiries are made, and it's confirmed that Shirley actually was in Williamson, the authorities will have no choice but to start a search for her. Because it's becoming clear as daylight to me now that something has happened to her.*

He got out of the car and shut its door, and then walked up to the motel's reception office.

CHAPTER 36

With his attention fully focused on the motel, Ted had no idea that he was being observed from just a short distance away. He didn't notice the car parked nearby, seemingly innocently, in the shadows.

Inside that car, May was watching his every move. She'd been waiting here for almost an hour, getting bored and wondering when Ted would arrive. She knew he would have to come here sooner or later; like she'd told him before, there was nowhere else nearby to room for the night.

As Ted stepped into the motel, May smiled at the selfie she'd taken with him at the tavern. Ted was cute . . . well, that was just too bad.

She frowned at her cellphone. Damn cell coverage was better out here that over in Williamson, but she'd been calling her father T-Bird for over an hour now, and couldn't get through to him. She wondered if that was because the signal had failed here too or because, like he sometimes did when he had important police business to attend to, T-Bird switched his phone off.

Feeling frustrated at not being able to make a report about Ted to her father, she intended to keep surveillance on the motel until she could.

CHAPTER 37

The motel's interior perfectly matched its exterior—it was run-down too. Ted had quickly accepted 'dilapidated' as being the pervasive residential theme around here.

The small loggy Ted stepped into was neat, but had clearly seen better days. Ted wasn't bothered. The bartender had warned him this was a shabby-looking place, so he had had no high expectations on his drive over. All he needed was somewhere to lay his head on a pillow and get some sleep.

A thin, dark-haired man was sitting behind the reception desk. He stood up when Ted entered.

"Hello, sir," he said with a smile. "I'm Roger. Can I help you?"

Ted nodded. "I'd like a room, please. Name's Ted Jamison."

Roger looked him over. Ted realized, that just like the patrons at the tavern where he'd recently met (and angered) that pretty girl May, Roger was assessing his smart designer suit and trying to place him. Ted figured that maybe hurrying off from work like he'd done hadn't really been the smartest move; he might have raised less attention here if he'd stopped at home first and changed his clothes to something more casual.

Roger nodded. "A room? Certainly, sir, although you look like you're used to more luxury than we offer. We're a very basic establishment. Unless . . . you are expecting a lady friend shortly?"

Ted quickly shook his head. "No, no . . . nothing like that, um . . . Roger. In fact . . ." Sighing, and feeling somehow defeated, he once more got out the photo of Shirley and handed it over the desk to Roger. "My fiancée is missing. I don't suppose you've seen her?"

He watched Roger take a really good look at the photo, speaking as he scrutinized Shirley's features: "Let's have a look-see. Hmmm. No, I don't recall her, myself, Mr. Jamison. But if you wait till later tonight, I'll ask my other staff member."

"All right. . . . thank you . . ." Ted said. Though he felt fresh disappointment, at least this Roger guy wasn't as uncommunicative (or in May's case, as unhelpful) as the some of the other people he'd asked.

"And . . ." Roger went on, "my mom comes over and cooks breakfast in the morning, so I can ask her then."

Ted nodded his gratitude, feeling once more, like he had outside in his car, that he was starting to get somewhere. Roger was clearly trying to be helpful.

"Thanks," he said. "It's just that I've drawn a blank everywhere else. I can't tell you . . ."

He broke off speaking and wiped his face, unable to hide his distress.

"Hey, man. Mr. Jamison . . ." Roger said gently.

"Ted. Call me Ted, please."

Roger nodded. "Okay, Ted. I can see how anxious you are. Take a seat. Lemme get you a coffee."

Ted sat himself on one of the chairs by the wall that Roger was pointing to. Roger then turned away from him to make his coffee, but kept speaking:

"How long ago has she been missing? Over the last week or two? I don't recollect anyone like her being here over that time. But if it was longer . . ."

Ted shook his head. "Yesterday . . ."

Roger frowned and eyed Ted curiously. Ted understood his look and tried to explain better:

"Look, I know that a day is a short time for a person to be missing," he said. "And you probably think it's crazy for me to be so worried . . . but this is totally unlike her. There's no sign of either her or the car. . . . No calls either."

Roger nodded, though he had a thoughtful look on his face. "Try to be positive. It's early days."

"It's just . . . We're real close," Ted went on. "We usually speak every few hours. But since yesterday . . . nothing. No answer from her to my calls or text messages."

"Well, if it's any consolation," Roger said while getting out a cup from a shelf in his desk, "Signal's bad over in the mountains, depending on which cellphone company you use. Only one cell tower reaches here and even that's pretty unreliable." He poured a stream of coffee into the cup and then went on: "So, tell me what's happened, that's got you so worried."

Ted shook his head. "That's what I don't understand; how anything *could* have happened. It was supposed to be a straightforward trip. Shirley was supposed to be home in time for a late dinner last night. But—I've heard nothing since she left Pittsburgh yesterday morning, before she drove over here . . . to the Ringo County Courthouse . . ."

Coffee in hand, Roger had been stepping out from behind the reception desk. But at Ted's mention of the courthouse, he stopped short and spilled the coffee in shock, splashing it on the floor and barely missing scalding himself. Ted thought the motel owner looked like he'd been hit by a bullet.

"The Ringo County Courthouse?" Roger asked slowly, his eyes beginning to narrow. Ted was surprised to see that the man had begun trembling.

"Yeah," Ted replied just as slowly. "Why? What's the matter?"

Roger seemed to recover his composure, but was still trembling. He passed Ted what remained of his coffee.

Ted nodded and accepted the cup from him; but by now his mind was a millions miles distant from drinking the steaming brew. Roger's strange behavior was communicating something bad to him, and he needed to know what it was.

"Do you know something?" Ted asked.

Roger sat down beside him and sighed. "Hey look, it might be nothing. I don't wanna alarm you."

Ted didn't think 'nothing' would have triggered such a reaction in Roger. When he'd first walked in here, the man had seemed calm, pleasant, and happy. And now, he looked as if the bottom of the world had just fallen out. "What? What is it?" he asked.

Roger didn't reply. He just studied Ted's face, his eyes foreboding and thoughtful. Ted had the strange and portentous feeling that the man was weighing up his strength of character.

"If . . . if you know something . . . Please . . . Tell me what you know," Ted pleaded with him.

Roger finally seemed to reach a decision. "Hmmm. Well . . . Alrighty." he said, then leaned forward in his chair and swiveled his body slightly so he was facing Ted.

"Your fiancée is missing. . . . And her car, you say?"

"Well, the car's actually mine, but yeah," Ted agreed.

"There's a chop shop a few ridges over, run by some bikers and vagrants," Roger said. "Reckon the car might have been stolen for parts."

Ted nodded, then shook his head as he digested the information: "But that makes no sense. She would have reported it—got in touch with me."

Roger looked at him coldly. "How can I put this? So, I'll just say it. Your girl might have gotten caught up in something."

"Something like what?" Ted asked him in breathless anticipation. He'd clearly come to the right place if he wanted information.

Roger sighed. "Word is, a couple of people have gone missing over there—I mean in the neighborhood of Williamson—in the last few months." He looked uneasily at Ted and continued: "But that's not the worst of it."

"Go on! What are you saying?" Ted asked impatiently.

Roger went on: "Well . . . people say it's some kind of cult that's responsible for the disappearing people."

"A religious cult?"

Roger laughed softly, a cold and flat sound. "Not any religion I know of. Unless you call devil-worship a religion."

Ted laughed nervously; this was becoming ridiculous. "Oh, come on!"

But Roger didn't backpedal and admit he'd merely been pulling Ted's leg. If anything his expression grew colder. "I'm serious. The chop shop out in the hills . . . They say demonic activity takes place there."

Ted gaped at him: "Whaaat!? You have got to be kidding me."

But Roger's face remained deadly serious, and he shook his head to counter Ted's statement. "Where there's smoke . . ."

"You think?" Ted was starting to understand that this really wasn't a joke; that Roger really meant what he was saying. *But it's impossible . . . impossible . . . !* He stood up and began pacing. "I've got to do something . . . call the police . . ."

But Roger's next comment punctured his motivation in that direction: "No good. Rumor has it that the sheriff is in on it."

Ted stared down at Roger. "The sheriff? How can that be?"

Roger shrugged in resignation. "Only ever spoke to him a coupla times myself, so can't comment firsthand. I only go by what people tell me. And they tell me he's corrupt; always into some scam or other. And . . . neck-deep into this cult himself. Why'd you think I looked so surprised when you mentioned that your fiancée went missing at the courthouse?"

Ted nodded slowly, remembering the inscription on the sign at the courthouse entrance. "Yeah, I get it now—the sheriff's office is in the courthouse building." He shook his head as if clearing it, and then added in a determined voice: "Well then, if the law won't help me, then I've got to find Shirley myself." He gazed at Roger. "Where is this place? This chop shop?"

Roger got to his feet. "Hey, wait up, there." Unsure of what he meant, Ted waited while Roger left him and walked off behind the reception desk again. Then Roger reached underneath the counter and pulled out a hunting rifle.

He regarded Ted with an icy smile. "We're going to need this. I wouldn't trust the sheriff." While still addressing Ted he picked up the receiver of the landline on the counter and dialed. "And I'm gravely concerned that your girlfriend is in mortal danger. Time is of the essence."

After gesturing to Ted to hold on, he spoke into the phone: "Maw? Can you cover for me? . . . Right now. Me and a friend are going huntin'."

Then Roger set the phone receiver back down in its cradle again. "That's settled then. We just need to wait a few minutes, until my mom arrives and then we can leave."

Ted nodded back at him. He was impatient to get going. He couldn't get Roger's statement that 'time was of the essence' out of his mind.

CHAPTER 38

May ducked down low inside her car when Ted and the motel owner emerged from the building. But not before she'd made out the clear shape of the hunting rifle that the motel owner clutched. Ted was holding something metal too, but she'd not been able to make out its shape—however it hadn't looked like a gun.

But one gun was enough to alarm her. And worse yet, both men had been walking purposefully and had looked grim-faced.

May kept her head down, biting her lip in frustration as she heard the sound of the motel owner's pickup truck start up, and then a few seconds later, heard the vehicle roll past her own. May still hadn't been able to raise her father on the phone and she was aware that things seemed to be getting of hand.

When she looked up again, she just made out the taillights of the pickup truck in the distance before it turned a curve in the highway and vanished from view, blocked out by the forest.

May had her suspicions as to where the pickup truck was headed; and they were troubling ones.

Cussing her father T-Bird under her breath for not picking up his phone, she started up her car and drove off, heading in the opposite direction from that in which the truck had gone.

There was clearly no time to waste here. No time at all.

CHAPTER 39

Clouds had covered the moon, leaving the Ringo County impound yard cloaked in darkness. Once more that darkness might have been absolute but for the flaming torches that wavered and flickered in it, giving the yard a hellish appearance.

Shirley was now coming to terms with the fact that her escape attempt had failed. The men who had come to her in the shed had since removed her from there, back to the space in the middle of the impound yard where yesterday they had defiled her. She was now incarcerated inside a large cage placed out in the open.

A number of the cultists lurked around the cage, but none came close to her or bothered her. Torches held in front of them, they huddled in groups and conversed in quiet tones, or sat and waited in silence, positioning themselves either on the ground or on the hoods of nearby cars. As time passed more and more cultists drove in and parked their cars or motorcycles.

Despite feeling defeated and in a state of delayed shock, Shirley once more tried to find her courage. To any casual observer, however, she was a dirty mess that sat silently and meekly on the floor of the cage and did her best not to attract attention to herself. She wished it was that simple, that she was merely having a nightmare or a lucid dream, that simply ignoring this situation would make it fade away from her.

The cage—her new prison—was high enough for her to stand up in. It stood right beside the same eerie structure she had noticed yesterday after her abduction. But now, both because she was sitting up and not lying on her back and also because tonight the lighting around here was brighter than it had been last night, Shirley was able to make more sense of the structure.

As best she could make of it from her (still restricted) vantage point, the weird structure was an altar made up of car parts and arcane artifacts that suggested devil-worship and black magic to her.

The topmost portion of the altar boasted a flat-topped table. This altar table had metal hoops at its corners through which ropes hung slackly to the floor. All of those dangling ropes that Shirley could see were stained red—and she wasn't about deceiving herself that the red coloring hadn't come from blood.

People—maybe even A LOT of people—have been sacrificed up there.

The clan cultists' altar was truly a weird amalgam. It was one of the strangest sights that Shirley had ever seen. At the point of the structure nearest to her, a mess of bones and feathers stuck out from what was clearly a stripped-down car engine. And next to the engine block, but in no logically related position to it, an animal skull—the skull of a wolf or a bear maybe—was mounted at the end of a steering wheel. And this was merely the portion of the construct that was closest to her. The 'altar' had car tires for steps, but these were covered with a rug of animal skins. It also had burning torches mounted in bone sconces sticking out of it. These torches were what provided the more brilliant and consistent illumination that she studied it by.

And then there were her captors themselves to consider; most of them once more clad in animal skins and with a few of them wearing bone headdresses. Shirley had quickly worked out that their skin garments were most likely provided by April's sister May.

She then remembered that strange half-beast half-female figure from yesterday. What, or rather *who* had that been? A woman dressed in furs? Or something more sinister and improbable? Looking out from her prison at the cult's female members, some of whom were fully clad in animal skins while others wore a mixed attire of fur and regular clothes as they waited for something that Shirley dreaded, she found it hard to separate actuality from make-believe. There was insanity in the air here—one look at the strange altar settled this in her mind.

This was a very crazy setup; one that she found almost impossible to accept as reality.

This can't be happening to me in the twenty-first century.

She sat there in reverie, unaware of her eyes closing as she hoped that Ted had begun looking for her. Her hope was tempered by the knowledge that her fiancé was unlikely to be able to find her in time; but at least it was something.

She felt a presence nearby, and next heard a voice:

"Hey there, ho! You're a damn lucky bitch, ya hear?"

Shirley opened her eyes to see Big Jim peering in through the cage bars at her. She ignored him, but that didn't prevent him from speaking anyway.

"Other bitches and bastards we got be dead by now, but we like you. You're somethin' else."

The fat man reached an arm in through the cage and tried to grab her, but the cage was a large one, and she was sitting just a little too far away for his dirty fingers to reach.

He laughed and the light from one of the torches mounted on the altar glinted off his bald head. "We got somethin' real special for you, girl. Just you wait till later tonight when the ritual commences."

Tears trickled down Shirley's face. She tried to stop them, but they just kept pouring out.

Big Jim laughed at her tears. "Me, I can't barely wait," he said with an expression of the evilest glee imaginable on his face.

Shirley kept weeping as he turned and waddled away from her.

CHAPTER 40

At the old farmhouse in the woods, Sheriff T-Bird was dozing peacefully in his favorite armchair when May burst into the house, her pretty face set in an expression close to panic.

May stood in the foyer for a few seconds catching her breath and then she hurried through the stacked piles of junk over to her father's side and began shaking his arm.

"Pappy! Why'n'tcha leave your goddamn phone switched on?" she complained as she shook him.

Still, despite the violence of her efforts, T-Bird took his sweet time with waking up. It had been a long and hard day for him and were it not for the clan ritual to be attended to tonight, he'd have preferred to have turned in right after dinner.

May, however, kept shaking him till he was fully awake. "Pappy, come on. Wake up! Work to do!"

T-Bird finally woke up enough to understand that his daughter needed his urgent attention. "Huh? What? What's the matter with you, girl?"

"Chick's boyfriend arrived in town, looking for her." May showed him her cellphone photo of Ted. "That's him. That's the guy. Damn lawyer, too. Checked into the Motor Lodge."

T-Bird nodded at her. "That so?"

May didn't think he understood the urgency of the situation. She grabbed his arm and began hauling him up out of his seat. "We gotta go, pappy."

T-Bird stared at her in surprise; the gravity of the situation was slowly beginning to get through to him. For one thing, May wasn't the kind of young woman who scared easily, and now she seemed really worried.

"What's your hurry?" he asked as he let her haul him to his feet.

May was pleased that she now had her father's full attention: "Him and the guy who runs the motel set off real fast in a pickup truck, and they was carrying a huntin' rifle."

T-Bird's eyes widened in alarm then. "Son-of-a-bitch!" Oh yes, May was right to be worried. It looked like they really did have a situation to handle now.

T-Bird set off hurriedly for the front door, then turned around to look at his daughter. "You comin' or what?"

May hurried over to join him and they rushed out of the farmhouse together and piled into his police cruiser, which then zoomed off between the pig pens and down the dirt road, heading for the highway.

CHAPTER 41

Roger parked his pickup-truck somewhere off a dirt road out in the woods. Then, with himself carrying the rifle and Ted bringing up the rear while carrying a set of bolt-cutters that belonged to Roger, the pair of them set off on foot from there.

Now that they were on their way to the impound yard, Ted was beginning to have reservations about accompanying Roger out here. What if this guy Roger was crazy, as nuts as those he claimed had abducted Shirley?

Because, so far I've only got this guy's word to go on. For all I know, the sheriff could be innocent and Roger the one who's actually in league with Shirl's abductors. If she actually has been abducted.

He didn't want to be unfair to Roger, but the guy struck him as being not exactly there in the head. During their drive from the motel to the woods, Roger had spoke of himself waging a one-man-army crusade of sorts against the cultists. 'Culling 'em' was how he'd put it, but it just sounded to Ted as if Roger been killing and burying these so-called 'cultists' each chance he got.

"Rumor has it that the cultists target out-of-towners . . . you know, folk that'll be hard to trace afterwards," Roger had explained in disgust; though now Ted was taking his words with more than just a pinch of salt.

He considered too the set of bolt-cutters Roger had made him carry, and could already see the local cops pressing charges of 'breaking and entering' against him.

Sure, Ted was willing to do whatever it took to save Shirley, but he wasn't looking to wind up inadvertently participating in a maniac's killing spree and then having the law prosecute him for mass murder.

"I dunno," he said now as they stalked quietly beneath the trees, "this all seems very strange to me."

"Shush," Roger instantly cautioned him. "I've told you there might be some of them around here." Then he pointed forward. "And we're just about arrived there now."

Ted looked forward. Yes, there was an impound yard out there in front of them. The yard lights were all off, but the moon was now out from amongst the clouds and, from where they stood the place looked like a giant parking lot, with possibly hundreds of vehicles of different brands and shapes and sizes arranged like toys inside a chain-link-fenced enclosure.

But there was also a strangeness to the impound yard.

"That's 'cos it's also a chop shop," Roger informed him when Ted questioned him about the weird piles of what seemed to be scrap junk that were dotted about the place. "What you're looking at is the stripped remains of cars. It's a great setup for them, because the sheriff's office are the ones who're supposed to investigate stolen cars anyway."

They snuck up closer to the impound yard. The woods ended about six feet from the chain-link fence, giving way to a grass boundary that extended inside the yard.

After a quick look up and down both ways, Roger handed his rifle to Ted and took the bolt cutters from him instead.

"Hide in here amidst the trees and keep watch for us, while I see to our way in," Roger instructed Ted. "The fence ain't electrified or anything like that, but there's usually guards around, though their patrols ain't regular. So just call me, or whistle like a bird if you spot anyone while I'm workin'."

Ted nodded. Roger seemed to have everything figured out. Ted kept out of sight while Roger snipped the wire fence open and then gestured to him to hurry over. They stepped through and then Roger tried to make the place he'd cut open look as undamaged as possible.

"Come on," he said, once he was done. "Keep your head down so no one can see you over the cars."

Ducking down low to indicate what he meant, Roger padded forward across the yard. Ted followed his lead and they made progress between the parked vehicles parked on the wide carpet of grass, some of which was quite high and gave the impression that the vehicles it grew beside had been stored in the impound for a long while.

They had to be careful, as the moonlight illuminated a good number of things around the compound this evening. For the moment, the clouds once more obscured the moon, but if they weren't careful, they'd easily be seen by the impound guards.

They hadn't gone very far into the yard when Ted tapped Roger on the arm to halt him.

Roger stopped and looked back inquisitively. Ted moved up to his side and first pointed at a small black sports car and then gestured to himself. "Over there—the black BMW—that's my car."

Roger moved nearer to him and nodded. "Okay, that's settled then. Meaning we're in the right place. Say, you believe me now?"

Ted nodded. "You were right. But where's Shirley?"

Disregarding Roger's instruction to keep his head down, he straightened up and began walking towards his car, but didn't get far before Roger grabbed him and held him back.

"Be careful, dammit. You can't just go storming in here. Go easy."

Ted nodded. He realized he'd let his worry get the better of him. Thankfully they'd been standing beside a large Yukon SUV at the time that provided good concealment. Once more ducking down, Ted followed Roger towards the middle of the yard.

"And watch your step—they set traps underfoot," Roger said over his shoulder.

Treading closer through the long grass under the partial cover of darkness, they approached something that Ted couldn't describe.

Roger had stopped on sighting that same exact thing in the clearing up ahead.

"What the hell is that?" Ted asked him in confusion. The thing was large, and although mostly obscured by shadows, the flaming torches stuck into its mass at intervals enabled him to make out some of its finer details: it seemed to be composed of crazily-juxtaposed car parts and animal bones. In some places, whole animal skeletons—several of those clearly rabbit remains, and one which seemed to have once been inside a wolf—were strung up on it.

"Roger, what the hell is that fucking thing?" Ted asked, feeling a deep chill settle over him as he posed the question.

Roger shrugged and then shivered. He looked confused too. "No clue. Except what I told you before. Fucking devil-worshippers?"

Ted nodded slowly. "Fuck." And now that he stared at the insane construct ahead of them, he could see that up on top of it—at the end of a short staircase paved with automobile tires and raised up on a trestle of metal legs—lay a flat surface that may or may not have once been the roof of a truck of some kind.

Is that thing an altar? If so it must be the most absurd altar in existence.

For the moment, however, Ted put his curiosity on hold. The sight of the strange 'altar' had rammed home to him the necessity of their locating and freeing Shirley as quickly as possible.

Roger was already heading away from him through the grass, and Ted hurried to catch up to him. But just as he reached him, Roger screamed in agony.

What? Ted looked down. There, concealed in the seemingly safe high grass, a bear trap had snapped shut around Roger's left ankle. The trap's vicious steel teeth had bitten deep into his flesh and Ted could see blood spilling over it.

While howling "Shit! Shit!" Roger was already falling to the ground and flinging his rifle away.

"Oh, fuck!" Ted said, knowing there was no way that anyone in the impound wouldn't have heard the noise, and that all hell was about to break loose.

CHAPTER 42

At the sound of the scream Shirley leapt up from the ground. She hurried over to the bars of the cage and peered out through them.

Oh, my God! she thought. A short distance away she saw Ted etched in the moonlight for a few seconds, before he ducked down out of sight. She was relieved that he didn't seem to be the one who'd screamed.

Ted's here! He's here! she thought in some relief, but then immediately realized that the cultists must have heard the noise too.

And she wasn't wrong. Scant seconds after the thought occurred to her, those cultists gathered by the altar were already looking around to locate the source of the screaming, with those who'd been sitting on the ground or on the hoods of cars, also leaping up or (in the latter case) down. In addition, several other clan members—Big Jim amongst them—came running out of the impound office to join them.

At first the cultists looked bewildered. A number of them even seemed to think that Shirley had been the one who'd screamed. But then, one of them (a weasely long-haired man whom she had heard the others call Leroy) pointed over between the cars, to right where she had just seen Ted duck down.

"Hey, over there!" Leroy shouted to the others. "Bear trap's caught us an intruder."

Her heart in her mouth as the chase began, Shirley too could see the man down in the long grass, struggling to remove the metal trap clamped onto his leg.

CHAPTER 43

Roger lay on the ground, panting in pain. His rifle lay about a yard away from him. He wasn't trying to reach it however; his attention was focused on his leg.

Ted knelt down beside Roger and tried to prize open the trap. He could hear the cultists behind him, closing in fast. He tried to tune them out and concentrate. He put his mind to the task and began separating the rusty metal jaws by forcing their springs down.

Then Ted felt Roger shoving him away. Roger winced in agony as the jaws of the trap snapped together again on his leg.

"No. Go! Save yourself! Run!" Roger told him.

Ted decided to do as he was told. He scrambled up to his feet. By then a large muscular man was already bearing down on he and Roger. And there were others following close behind that one.

"Quick! Go!" Roger repeated, his voice insistent.

Ted nodded and dashed off between two nearby cars. Keeping his head down, he quickly retraced the path they had followed through the impound yard. He looked back once and saw that he wasn't being pursued. Apparently, the devil worshippers had all gathered around Roger.

Ted dashed through the hole in the fence and took shelter in the woods again.

CHAPTER 44

Roger nodded to himself, satisfied that Ted had at least escaped. Though the clan cultists had caught him, his death here wouldn't be for nothing. He expected Ted to soon have the authorities out here—the *real* authorities, not T-Bird's crooked cronies. That at least was something to look forward to.

And even in his current dire straights—and the agony of the trap biting into his leg—Roger took some pride in his achievements. For the past year he'd given The Clan—that was what these sickos called themselves: 'The Clan'—well, yeah, he'd given them a run for their money. He'd killed a whole lot of them—he'd actually lost count of the number of their dead—and they'd never figured out he was the one picking them off one at a time.

Roger looked up then. That greasy bastard Leroy—the fucker who helped Buffalo run the chop shop—was staring down at him with an ugly frown on his ugly face. Roger wished he could just shoot Leroy, blow the son-of-a-bitch right off the surface of this earth.

And while there's life there's hope, right? Roger reached over towards his rifle, but—fuck—it was too far away. He sighed in regret when Leroy picked up the rifle instead.

Roger suddenly felt sad. This shouldn't have to end like this. He began wondering who'd look after his aged mother once he was dead.

CHAPTER 45

After a while of wondering what to do now, Ted decided there was no way he could possibly help Roger at the moment, and that his best course of action would be to drive back to the motel and try to find help there.

That decided, he tried to retrace his way back through the woods to where Roger had parked his pickup truck. Roger had thoughtfully left his keys in the truck's ignition in case they needed to make a fast getaway.

After a few minutes of walking, however, Ted had to admit that he was lost.

But at least, he was close to a dirt road, and now the impound yard was far behind him, nowhere in sight.

He set off walking down the dirt road in the direction of the highway, hoping to find someone to give him a lift over to the motel.

His worries that he might be too far away from civilization and also that this might be too late at night for any vehicles to drive out this way were cut short a short while later, when he saw a car's headlights approaching.

Relieved, Ted stepped out into the road and began waving his arms at the oncoming car to halt it.

CHAPTER 46

Shirley stood in the cage with her hand pressed over her mouth, staring at the distant shadows beyond the impound yard into which Ted had just disappeared. She hadn't actually seen him exit the yard; but she assumed that was the way he had gone.

"Oh, Ted," she whispered at the darkness.

Then she noticed one of her captors staring at her. Shirley thought this particular madman was named Buffalo. As far as Shirley could tell, 'Buffalo' was the one in charge of the impound yard.

Her fears that he'd noticed the direction of her gaze were confirmed when he grinned and turned away from her and then, after gesturing to get the others' attention, pointed directly where she'd been staring.

"Over there!" he directed them. "He went that way!"

The mob of clans-folk split into two groups; half of them headed off through the cars, looking for Ted.

The remaining clan members surrounded Ted's partner, with Buffalo walking halfway across to them from Shirley's cage.

Shirley winced as she watched two of the clan roughly heave Ted's friend to his feet. She'd not seen the man before tonight, but she appreciated his coming out here to help rescue her.

The man howled in agony as the clan manhandled him. The bear trap was still clamped around his ankle and one of the men kicked the trap so that its jaws clamped even tighter into his flesh. There was no way he'd be able to stand up if he wasn't being supported.

Shirley gasped as Leroy aimed a rifle into the man's face.

No! she thought desperately as the captive gabbled something at Leroy. His actual words were indistinguishable from this distance, but she had the distinct impression he'd said "Fuck you!" He'd been smiling anyway. She was certain of this.

Next thing Shirley knew, Leroy angrily stuck the barrel of the rifle in the stranger's mouth and pulled the trigger. Shirley flinched at the gunshot, and then watched as the stranger fell down dead.

Realizing that she'd just witnessed a murder being committed, Shirley slumped forward against the bars of her cage feeling distraught.

Then she noticed that the clansmen were returning towards the altar and the cage. Leroy was conferring with Buffalo as they approached her.

Shirley felt a sudden burst of hope—almost of joy, in fact. *Oh, they don't look pleased—I think Ted must have escaped from them.*

Then she noticed Buffalo once again staring at her suspiciously, and her happiness vanished like salt dissolved in water. Buffalo was tall and as bearded and mustached as Big Jim, but where Big Jim was bald and most of his bulk was flab, Buffalo had a full head of black hair, seemed years younger by comparison, and was also quite muscular. In the right circles he might even have been considered handsome.

"What else you seen, girl?" Buffalo asked her in a nasty voice.

Shirley refused to be intimidated by him. "Nothing. . . . just looking. Who was that you people just killed?"

"Motel guy," Buffalo replied sullenly. "He's an asshole. Though why you want to know, I have no idea."

Shirley nodded her head in acknowledgement, and almost smiled in relief. She now realized that April and May had disparaged the motel owner simply because they didn't like him. *They* were the crazy ones, not he. She looked across at the man's corpse, and frowned. Then she half-smiled at Buffalo again. At least Ted had escaped from them—it wasn't *his* corpse out there on the grass with a hole blown in its head.

Buffalo was still scowling at her with a wary look in his eyes. But then he looked beyond her and smirked. "Now, maybe *that's* something to wipe the smile off of your face, coming up here, right now."

The evil man seemed so pleased that Shirley had to see what he was referring to. She swung around, and her face instantly dropped.

Oh, no!

May was marching Ted towards them at gunpoint. Ted's hands were cuffed behind him and the crooked sheriff T-Bird followed behind them both, a grim look on his face.

"Ted! Ted!" Shirley shrieked. Her emotions were a mingled cocktail of delight that he was now here with her, relief that he was safe, and also horror that he'd been caught too.

Ted looked scared, but behind his mask of fear, Shirley could see his own delight and relief at finally finding her. "Shirley, you're safe!" he said. "Thank God!"

"Ain't no God in it, fool," May said in a scornful voice. "We don't believe in that fella. We got us our own beliefs."

"How'd you find him, T-Bird?" Big Jim asked. "We saw him come in here with the motel guy, but then he ran off—we've men out combing the woods for him right now."

T-Bird smiled coldly. "We *didn't* find him—he found us. Dumb son-of-a-bitch jumped out into the road in front of our car and flagged us down for help."

Shirley couldn't believe their bad luck. *Ted escaped only to run into the very people he was fleeing from?*

"And so we decided to do our citizenly duty and bring him back here to be reunited with his girlfriend," T-Bird finished with a cruel laugh.

Big Jim laughed too, as did several of the other cultists.

Ted refused to be cowed. "Now, look here. Let us go and we can sort this all out. I can get you a plea bargain if . . ."

Though Shirley appreciated the fact that Ted was trying to get the clan to set them free, she doubted that they would be interested in any kind of bargaining, and she was quickly proved right when May threw back her head and laughed.

"Enough talk, law-boy," May said. Then she nodded to her father. "Put the gag in his mouth."

Shirley watched Sheriff T-Bird roughly gag Ted.

Once that was done, May shrugged at Ted. "See? No God, no law. I brung you to the clan for them to decide your fate. What say you, people?"

The air was now filled with a hubbub of bloodthirsty cries, with people raising their torches high as if protesting with them. Amongst the chorus of loud voices a few specific statements were discernible:

"Sacrifice him!" Buffalo shouted.

"Death to him!" Leroy screamed.

"Kill! Kill! Kill!" was Big Jim's loud contribution, which made Shirley hate him even more than she already did.

May held her hands up for silence and everyone instantly quietened down. Shirley was surprised by this—the purple-haired young woman appeared to be in control of them all, even of her own father; who now seemed as deferential to her instructions as the rest of them, as evidenced by how he'd quickly responded to her instruction to gag Ted.

May sneered. "Seems like the clan has spoken. And we have a consensus of opinion. Sacrifice it is. Death to the lawman!"

Shirley instantly screamed: "No! No! Please, no!"

May looked slyly sideways at her, and said pointedly: "And since this is his lover, I am sure she will just *love* to watch what we do to him."

"No! No!" Shirley protested. She stared at Ted.

Ted looked dumbfounded at this situation they'd found themselves in. He was staring back at her with questions in his eyes. "Sacrificed? What the hell?" his gaze asked.

"Prepare the altar for the sacrifice," May told the clan.

"No! Stop!" Shirley shrieked.

"Oh, hush your mouth or I'll shut it for you," May said nastily. Then she stepped up close to the cage and Shirley and hissed between the bars, in a voice scarcely louder than a whisper: "You're making us women look weak, with your sniveling and helplessness. It's not attractive, you know. Get a grip. Men may think they rule the roost, but we all know there's a limit to what a cock can do."

Shirley just stared at her, unable to think straight. In fact, so dumbfounded was she by what was going on, that the possibility of violence never occurred to her. She was standing close enough to May to reach her through the bars of the cage and at least attempt to choke her to death or break her neck, or at the very least punch her. But she made no attempt to reach or attack May. Her attention was concentrated on Ted, and on the clan, who stood motionless around him, but seemed mere seconds away from performing devilish acts on his person.

May, however, seemed to have slipped into a sort of daydream. She was practically talking to herself while gazing into the distance:

"Women have the power," she said coldly, "and these clansmen know that, ultimately. But you gotta earn their respect first. Then they will worship you!"

Her trance faded and her attention snapped back to Shirley: "Well, not actually worship *you*," she whispered. "But they will do *my* bidding."

Then she stepped away from the cage and began giving instruction: "Fetch that body you left over there and use it for pig food," she instructed a group of fur-decorated men.

The men instantly scurried off—fur-covered as they were, they looked very much like rats, Shirley thought—to fetch the murdered man's body.

But . . . I'm missing two people here, she suddenly realized. *Where are both April and her mother? Or aren't they meant to be part of this craziness?* Looking around, however, she couldn't catch sight of the sheriff's wife and other daughter.

May now addressed the rest of the cultists. "Prepare the sacrifice," she ordered. "We will party and play, and very soon too. Let the ritual commence!"

These cultists—her father T-Bird leading the way—now burst into motion also, grabbing the struggling Ted and manhandling him away from Shirley and towards their crazy half-machine, half-skeleton altar, and then up its fur-carpeted tire steps.

A chilling smile on her beautiful face, May returned her attention to Shirley:

"You two are not the first tortured lovers in the world," she said. "But you *will* both soon feel the extremity of exquisite pain—in mind, body and spirit."

Then she flung up her arms, and as playful as a child with a new toy, strutted off into the darkness.

CHAPTER 47

As Ted was dragged up onto the strange altar, the sound of tribal drums erupted from somewhere on its other side. Shirley was too focused on what was happening to her boyfriend to at first notice the drumming, but she soon became aware of both its percussive rhythms and of the steady chanting of voices around her. The cultists, flaming torches held high, were droning a low and chilling monotone.

And then it was her own turn. On May's instructions, she was dragged out of the cage.

"Let me go!" she howled at them. But instead of this, the four men who'd pulled her out of the cage now manhandled her over towards a stout wooden pole that she'd so far not noticed because it was situated near the far side of the altar.

As the men bound Shirley to this pole, she was distracted from her woes by the sight of another set of cult members carrying the motel owner's corpse past the altar towards a deeper part of the yard. She remembered May instructing them to "feed his body to the pigs." That must be where they were headed then: over to the pig pens beside her prison cell.

Then the corpse bearers vanished between the vehicles and she was once more left with her own troubles.

She wrestled against the ropes and duct tape she'd been secured with, trying to break free. But it was hopeless, and she soon gave up. She realized that even if she did somehow miraculously free herself, she had no way to escape the fur-clad men and women who surrounded her. And the dead motel owner was a clear testament to how far they would go to ensure her silence.

So instead, she stared up at Ted. He lay spread-eagled and naked on the altar, his hands and feet tied to its corners by those same stout bloodstained cords that she had earlier observed, and his mouth bound in a gag of filthy fabric material. He struggled violently, but had no leeway for any effective movement, since all four of his limbs were stretched taut.

A woman was dancing around the altar, whipping Ted with a length of rubber cord, possibly a wire. Her body swayed like grass in a storm. After she had completed a full circuit of the altar, she reached down to Ted's crotch and grabbed his penis. Then, while gazing down at Shirley and making eye contact with her, she began making masturbatory movements on the limp penis, jerking it up and down. Shirley grimaced as Ted's eyes widened in apprehension. Having herself suffered sexual abuse at the hands of their captors, she understood how he felt; it was terrifying to be violated like this, more so before a public audience.

She stared at him, trying to lock her gaze with his, but she and he were both positioned at relative angles to each other that made this impossible.

Around her the clan members were grinning and chanting as they watched the dancer sexually molest Ted while her own eyes glittered with lewdness and amusement. Their eyes were wide with excitement, and their horrible singing intensified and grew louder.

"We take their strength and we take their spirit!" they wailed in unison. "With their life-force taken and added to our strength, our life-force grows more powerful!"

Shirley began wondering if they were collectively on narcotics. She'd so far seen no evidence of ritual drug use, but they might have done so before fetching her from the prison hut.

But then, while Shirley tried to deduce whether the cultists were high or not, there was a collective gasp of intense excitement from them. An 'Oooh' of pleasure that spread from the front to the rear of the insane congregation, and which forced Shirley to follow the direction of their gaze back up to the altar again.

She gasped at the sight that beheld her there. A second woman had emerged from the rear of the altar, possibly through the 'curtain' of hubcaps that were still swaying behind her, with their silver surfaces reflecting the flames.

So, no, I didn't hallucinate her last night!

It was the woman-beast figure from the previous night's ritual celebration. The one who had lingered here for just a little while; too short a period for Shirley to see her clearly. Shirley's later intense suffering and trauma had since reduced this woman's existence and importance to nothing, making her seem more of a figment of her tortured imagination than a creature of flesh and blood. And later, in her bid to dig her way out of her prison, she had completely forgotten about her. But now, Shirley saw that this new female was both a solid presence and apparently a very important one indeed.

Shirley figured this woman had to be a high priestess of some kind. Now that her view was unobscured by moving bodies, she also understood why last night the woman had seemed to her to be partly animal.

Most of her head was concealed by a horrifying half-mask with long bunny ears that only revealed her mouth and chin. Her attire was partially similar to that of the other cultists. She wore a skimpy leather-and-fur outfit, like a two-piece swimsuit made of fur. But unlike the others, she also wore fur gloves that reached her elbows, and fur boots that reached her knees. Both her gloves and her boots ended in sharp 'claws' made of bone.

She carried a scary weapon: a club made from an aluminum baseball bat, but with its business end heavily spiked with large metal projections.

The overall effect of the woman's presence was a chilling and powerful one and Shirley felt both impressed and cowed.

At the priestess's appearance a hush had settled over the congregation.

"Behold the Wolf-Rabbit deity Oryctolupus," the woman masturbating Ted sang to them, and their silence instantly turned to loud applause. The woman's ceaseless attention to Ted's genitals had by now borne fruit—he'd gotten an erection. Shirley didn't feel offended by this; she merely felt sorry for Ted.

The 'Wolf-Rabbit Deity' moved sensuously, waving her club in the air and dancing her way back and forth across the altar. But her motions were clearly a show of her power and dominance; there was very little eroticism in the way she swayed as she approached Ted.

Remembering May's earlier 'female-empowerment' rant to her, Shirley wondered if perhaps she was the one beneath the grotesque rabbit-head mask. The body size and shape looked just about right. But no, May had had purple hair, and from what little Shirley made out of the hair of this so-called 'Wolf Rabbit Deity,' this woman had dark hair.

Maybe it's her sister April then, or maybe their mother; though Star was a little thickset.

The woman hand-pumping Ted's penis now removed her hand from him and stepped back, giving the priestess free access to his body. Then, after accepting the woman's scary club from her and placing it on a shelf made from intertwined windshield wipers, she assisted the priestess on climbing on top of Ted.

Once the 'goddess' had straddled Ted's hips, the chanting increased, growing louder and faster. And now everyone was singing a single word: "Rape! Rape! Rape!"

The 'rape' chant beat against Shirley's mind with invisible fists. She wished she could shut her ears as she watched the priestess abuse Ted. Yes, she wanted to shut her eyes, but something about the performance up on stage—and also a strange terror that if she even blinked or looked away for a second, she was certain to miss something devastatingly important—compelled to keep watching her fiancé's degradation at the priestess's hands.

She—the Wolf-Rabbit Deity—was strong and powerful; there was no doubt about that. She rode Ted in rhythm with the mob's chanting, which slowly metamorphosed into guttural 'ugh' sounds and groans of ecstasy. The other woman stood watching with approval, intense lust written all over her face.

Shirley watched Ted as the priestess used him to satisfy her carnal urges; Ted looked traumatized. Despite the woman's good figure—she had large breasts—her mask and apparel made her look so grotesque that no one—except maybe one of her own deranged followers—could possibly consider her sexually attractive.

Shirley suddenly found herself screaming and crying, but her anguish and protests were lost amidst the greater commotion.

And then, suddenly, when the noise around her had become so deafening that she wondered how the rest of the world didn't hear it and come running to save Ted and herself, the cultist's goddess representative flung back her head and growled out a violent and loud orgasm. And then she grabbed an ornate blade from the hands of the other woman up on the dais with her.

Raising the ceremonial knife high with both hands, she plunged it down and stabbed Ted. It seemed as if she had hit him directly in the heart. Blood burst out of him like a fountain and drenched her.

"God, noooo!" Shirley screeched in utter disbelief, feeling crazy with distress.

The blood-spattered 'deity' grinned and climbed down off Ted.

And then, as if she'd given them an unheard signal, the clan went wild. They swarmed forward past Shirley, who was shoved left to right on the pole as the mob rushed up onto the altar.

Weeping and screaming, she watched the mob reach Ted, whose jetting blood was running off the altar into a series of channels that fed a wide trough in which the blood pooled.

And then like wild beasts—like ravaging wolves—the cultists fell upon Ted, who thankfully already seemed to be dead.

It was a feeding frenzy. Flying arcs of blood and shredded body parts flashed into view and vanished again. Some clan members scooped up Ted's blood in their hands and brought those hands to their mouths to drink it. Others, who were more frenzied, plunged their faces into the trough and drink the blood directly. Sheriff T-Bird was one of these latter; and now Shirley finally saw Star. The sheriff's wife was standing by Ted's left leg, covered in blood, and holding a shining hatchet.

And throughout this insanity, there was music in the air: the throbbing syncopated beat of tribal drums that formed a demonic foundation to the whooping and orgiastic screaming.

Shirley continued screaming too. She tugged at her restraints wildly. In her worst nightmares she could never have expected what she was watching.

A flurry of blades—axes, hatchets, kitchen knives. Ted's corpse their target. Each blade going in clean and coming out bloodied, some with flecks of fat and flesh attached to their reddened metal.

The love of her life being butchered like he was one of the sheriff's hogs.

"Stop! Stop! Stop it!" she cried out, whimpering in almost psychotic distress.

The mob of cultists around Ted parted slightly, and Shirley's eyes locked on Buffalo. The heavily bearded man was working intently on dismembering Ted's right leg from its hip joint socket with a butcher's knife, stripping the flesh from the bone and digging deep into the obstructing muscle and severing the connecting ligaments.

Then someone held out a plastic sack with its neck open, and pieces of flesh, skin and bone flew through the air, half-filling it.

Most of the cultists had satisfied their blood craving now. With crimson-stained mouths and bodies, they drifted down from the altar and turned the ceremony back over to the priestess and her assistants.

Shirley gasped at her sight of Ted's body now. For the most part he'd been stripped down to the bone, with literally barely enough flesh left to cover those bones. His bloody ribs curved over an empty space, both his lungs and heart having been removed and either eaten or placed in the plastic bag the assistant had been holding.

Overcome by the insanity of it all, Shirley abruptly stopped screaming and just stared. She wondered how she hadn't yet fainted.

Numb, she watched as the woman who'd masturbated Ted to erection now pushed a finger into his right eye socket and hooked out his eyeball, extending it as far as it would stretch on its string of nerve fiber.

Finally, while laughing uproariously, the woman snapped the eyeball off of its nerve connections and then to the mild applause of the other cultists, bit into it. The eyeball squirted out a jello-like substance that shone on her mouth like lip gloss.

Beside her, the priestess stood in a strong and confident stance, her hands on her hips, her lips curved upward in a broad smile beneath her rabbit mask. The assistant who had collected Ted's flesh in a bag was now daubing the priestess's body with blood. He was using an animal's foot as his paintbrush, and was pressing the foot against her rather than smearing her with it, so that she was imprinted with the beast's footprints. He coated her thighs and belly and her throat like this. It was a horrible effect, one intensified by the effect of the blood dribbling down from the bloody smudges, but for the most part its scariness was lost on Shirley.

When the assistant had gotten through also coating her back with the animal footprints made from Ted's blood, she dismissed him and then swung around and once more surveyed the corpse.

The 'Wolf-Rabbit Deity' turned away from the ravaged corpse. The last of the cultists were now stepping down from the altar, and as they departed and left her alone up there, she the priestess fixed her stare on Shirley. She retrieved her wickedly spiked metal club from the floor and pointed it at Shirley.

Shirley saw her mouth tighten in a grin of triumph.

But oh, you've not won yet, bitch!

Shirley's eyes locked with the murderess's, and it was then, realizing what she'd just lost and who had done it to her, that her emotional state went through a hundred-and-eighty-degree shift. Suddenly she no longer felt scared, or even saddened . . . or even traumatized anymore. All that Shirley Wade now felt in her heart was pure unadulterated rage towards all of these lunatics who'd perpetuated this atrocity against she and Ted.

Rage and hatred.

Although tears still stained her face, her heart hardened with resolve. *Oh, this isn't over yet. Not if I can help it!*

ACT THREE:
HELL HATH NO FURY

CHAPTER 48

It was much later now. The atrocities of the night lay only in the shadows of memory; and those who would remember them positively had left and gone to bed.

The impound yard was still and silent in the darkness.

And then out in the pig pen near Shirley's prison, the pigs began squealing.

Shirley, who had been locked up in the same wooden shack again after watching Ted's murder, was bent over the hole she was excavating in the hut floor. Still numb after what she'd earlier witnessed, she nevertheless worked with a ruthless fury, attacking the soil with the nail and a flat piece of wood she'd unearthed across the shed at the expense of getting several splinters stuck in her palms. Working relentlessly in the shed's dark interior, she attacked the floor as if it was responsible for Ted's death.

Her face was moist with tears and her heart felt empty; her hopes had been summarily ravaged and demolished. She had already revisited her suspicion that the priestess—the murderess who'd robbed her of the man she'd wanted to spend the rest of her life with—was either April or her sister May, neither of whom she'd noticed amongst the other cultists once the outrage had commenced. If Shirley made it out of this mess alive, those two crazy bitches would answer to her for what they'd done.

(As touching questions of what crazy religion the cultists actually practiced, Shirley was still too mentally distressed to assemble those scattered fragments of their theological conversations she'd overheard into any sort of irrational whole that made sense out of her captors' nonsense. She'd heard their claim to worship a goddess named Oryctolupus; who was somehow personified in the murderous priestess with the furry bikini and the rabbit-head mask. *Who was Oryctolupus supposed to be? A mad version of the Easter bunny perhaps?*)

The hole in the floor was considerably larger now, almost as large as she needed it to be, and Shirley was desperate to finish it quickly, tonight if possible, because otherwise she wasn't sure how she would hide it from notice the next time the cultists visited her. The fact that the cultists hadn't seen fit to use her as a sex toy tonight meant she had more strength to dig with. She had expected them to rape her again, but it hadn't happened; Ted's unexpected capture and death seemed to have satisfied their bloodthirstiness and thus spared her their evil attentions.

The pigs were still squealing.

Shirley was completely focused on her digging and so at first she ignored the noise of the pigs. She thought that maybe they'd smelt a wolf or a bear in the woods outside the yard—the hog pen was very close to the perimeter fence.

But the sound of pig squealing continued; in fact, it was growing louder. And now it clearly wasn't so much that the hogs were alarmed as that they were excited about something.

So, wiping sweat from her forehead, Shirley paused her digging, knelt up from the hole in the ground, and listened.

Yes, there definitely was something odd about the racket the pigs were making.

Shirley scrambled up off the ground and pressed her face against the crack between the wall planks that faced their direction, and peered through it at the pig pen.

Now that their murderous ritual ceremony was concluded the clan had turned the lights in the impound yard back on. And so, Shirley discovered that she had a ringside seat to yet another outrage. Leroy was standing beside the pig pen. The tall and skinny man was holding a bloodstained sack. Shirley's suspicion about the sack's contents was confirmed a few seconds later, when Leroy pulled out a handful of chopped meat and tossed it over the pen's wooden railing to the swine.

Then he reached into it again, pulled out half of a human hand and flung that over the railing as well.

The squealing racket increased in volume. The pigs went into a frenzy as they devoured Ted's bloody flesh.

Inside the shed, her face and body pressed against the planks, Shirley began sobbing as she watched Ted's body get fed to the pigs.

Leroy laughed. "Heard tell that was a lawyer, boys," he informed the pigs in his high-pitched drawl. "Make sure you suck him dry. He's likely bled other folks dry too. Tch! Law man, huh? Don't you hogs even spit out the bones, you hear?"

This was too much: Shirley's numbness dissolved in a flash and she was instead overcome by a burst of the most intense nausea imaginable. She staggered away from the crack and threw up in the nearest corner; the one a short distance away from her hole. She stood there trying to get a grip on herself, wiping her mouth with the back of her hand and panting.

Outside, she heard Leroy leaving the now raucous pig pen and wandering off again, with the additional sounds of him crinkling up the now presumably empty plastic sack while humming to himself in satisfaction.

She waited until the sound of his footsteps had faded and she could no longer hear his voice, then she scooped up some water from the water bucket and rinsed out her mouth, spitting the bitter vomit onto the mess in the corner.

Then she returned to the hole she was excavating and, with a frenzied and desperate expression on her face, resumed her frantic digging.

CHAPTER 49

At the center of the impound yard all was peace and quiet now. Silence prevailed, except for the distant porcine squealing.

Star and April were working around the altar, cleaning up. Star was busy removing some decorative dangling bones that were tied to car parts.

The mother-daughter duo had been hard at work for a while, as evidenced by the bottles of bleach and cleaning equipment lying around. The altar still looked weird, but it no longer looked like someone had been murdered on it.

Star smiled to herself; the altar actually didn't look so strange in broad daylight. With the sun out, this hallowed place of worship was just another mass of scrap—the table on which victims were sacrificed folded away like a foldable bed and the myriad wolf and rabbit skins that covered the steps were no longer in evidence, having been packed up and stored in boxes like the one April was currently filling up with stuff. The filled boxes were hidden away by Buffalo and Leroy until they were required again.

Still, an explanation for the unwieldy pile of metal in the middle of the impound yard did occasionally need to be tendered to those who came to retrieve their vehicles from here, and also to the occasional authorities who sometimes stopped by the place. The explanation Buffalo gave them was that the altar was a giant sculpture he was working on; something that celebrated 'the fusion of man and machine.' He also said he hoped to sell it someday, which always left the visitors nonplussed and thinking he was mad.

Star laughed at the comedy of it all. *If only they knew,* she thought.

And then she sighed. It had been ages since she'd officiated as Wolf-Rabbit Deity, as the goddess Oryctolupus incarnated in human flesh. She missed the rush of it—the violence and the sexuality of the sacrifices . . . She smiled down at April.

It's wonderful that my two daughters—my own flesh and blood—are the leaders of the clan now.

April was fiddling about inside a box, adjusting the bones and decorations packed in it.

"Jus' like Christmas," Star told her, a smile on her attractive middle-aged face. "Time to take the decorations down. Till next time."

"Yeah, it is," April nodded through a tired smile. "I'm gonna get off home now, mamma. You know I'm due in at work in a few hours."

"Sure, honey," Star generously replied after placing two rabbit skulls side-by-side in a large carton. "You must be tired an' I know it's a workday. Most of the clan done left now anyhow. Couple that still remains is slumberin'."

"Seen May?" April asked. "She need a ride home?"

Star nodded and gestured around the impound yard, at no particular location. "May's still around someplace, restin' up. She's had a real busy night, too, as you well know. Your pappy's in the office with your Uncle Jim. So, if you're leavin' now, best you go by yourself. We'll follow you on home, there, soon."

That said, she wound the string of a bone decoration around her hands and placed it neatly in the box April was holding.

"Okay, that's the last one. All set. There you go. Bye, now."

"Thanks. See you later, mamma," April said, shutting the box. Then she turned and carried it off towards the impound office.

Star looked away from her daughter and saw Leroy approaching, carrying the empty plastic sack that had borne the dead lawyer's remains.

Leroy grinned at her. "Them hogs sure do like human food."

Star chuckled. "Leroy, they gets human food all the time—leftovers, cabbage, beans and stuff. What they *really* like is humans *as* food!"

"Yup, that's what I meant," Leroy agreed, and Star could see that he was keeping a straight face with difficulty. "They like *beans*. Human beans!"

They both burst out laughing.

"Hope you weren't rootin' for any leftovers to take home for the rest o' your hogs on the farm. I just tossed it all in, and they're all squabblin' over the choice cuts right now." He rattled the empty plastic sack in the air. "See? Empty!"

Star scowled at him.

"You know I know the drill, Leroy. T-Bird told us all often enough: No removal of incriminating evidence off-site. Clean up after ourselves. Get rid of all the evidence. Why d'ya think I tidy this place better'n I clean up my own house? Think I'm a natural-born bleach queen? No way." She frowned. "And you—don't forget to burn that damn sack."

Leroy smirked back at her. Star thought he looked a bit riled, but if he felt upset, well that was his own damn fault. Leroy had started it by suggesting that she might be sloppy and take some slops (she almost laughed at the pun) home for the hogs.

"You're preachin' to the choir, ma'am," Leroy said. "I bin part of this clan long enough. Boy and man. Generation after generation."

Star shrugged. "Jus' sayin'."

Leroy gestured towards the office. "Others still sleepin' it off?"

"Yup," Star replied. "Just you and me still workin'. Buffalo drove Darlene home a short while ago. Said he'd finish the night over at her place."

Leroy looked disgusted. "Tch. Typical. Right, I'm just gonna go do some checking up on stuff." He pointed over to where April was just getting into her Kia hatchback. "And once April's gone, I'll go back and lock the main gate again. Least, until you're ready to drive out." he grinned at her. "And I *will* burn the evidence—as you so rightfully recommended."

"Yeah. But make sure you secure the perimeter fence again too, till them hogs do their job."

Leroy gave her a pissed off look. "Like I said, you can't teach an old dog old tricks—cos I know them already. Bin doing this for years, Star." But then, he seemed to notice something bothersome in her gaze, because his face lost its irritation and his expression turned questioning instead. "Why you keepin on at me, chewin' on my ear, Star?"

She sighed. "I do apologize to you, Leroy. I dunno . . . I'm kinda jumpy. On edge. I just have this funny feelin' in my gut."

Leroy laughed. "Me, too. Hunger, I calls it."

But Star shook her head emphatically. "No. Somethin' more 'n that. I dunno . . . I feel kinda spooked." And she meant it. She could feel 'something' in the air, something that wasn't just the cold which was beginning to settle over the impound yard as night approached morning. She felt an unease, as if something somewhere was wrong, but what could that thing possibly be?

Spooked? For a moment Leroy looked surprised at what she'd just told him. However, his first attempt to reply her was interrupted for a few seconds by the noise of April starting up her car and reversing it out of parking.

But once April was driving off, Leroy raised his hands over his head and scrunched up his face, monster like, at Star. "Mu-wah-ha-ha-haaa!" he growled in a ludicrous TV monster voice that made Star burst into smiles.

Leroy turned and lurched off like Frankenstein's monster, leaving Star shaking her head and grinning quietly to herself. Yeah, Leroy was right, there were no monsters out here.

No one except ourselves, maybe. But we're only monsters to those who aren't part of the Clan—to infidels who don't revere the goddess Oryctolupus.

Feeling much better, she picked up a cleaning cloth and wiped it over the altar top. A short while later she was working contentedly again on the massive metal stage.

CHAPTER 50

It took a while to get it done and at one point, she felt so exhausted that she was about to give up and lay down and sleep, but finally Shirley finished digging her hole.

Kneeling at its edge, she peered down into the wide dark space she'd cleared by the wall.

Inside the hole, the bases of a couple of the upright wall planks were exposed. Shirley reached down and got a good grip on these, and then she began to forcefully manipulate them, pulling and shaking them in an attempt to further loosen them.

Now that she'd almost achieved her objective, she felt much stronger. She was imbued with extra determination. *So long as my luck holds, with just a little more effort I'll be out of this fucking shack.*

Using her feet and legs to get leverage, she strained to rip the planks off of the nails that secured their upper lengths. With her whole body extended, she pushed and forced the planks until she heard that first dull 'Crack.'

Scared that the noise might have been heard down in the center of the impound yard and might bring someone over to check on what she was up to, she froze for a while. But then she relaxed and realized she was worrying for nothing. Nearby, the pigs were making a lot more noise than she was. Anyone paying attention from far away was certain to ascribe any sounds he heard solely to the unruly swine.

So, reassured now and reinvigorated by the closeness of her release, Shirley continued worrying at the planks. She was greatly encouraged by the rush of air through the widening space and the increasing looseness of the planks each successive time she shook them.

And then suddenly, it was over. One final wrench and two slats of wood pulled free of the wall at once, leaving a gap big enough for her to get through.

She sat back and took some time to collect herself. Then she peeked out of the hole in the wall and looked carefully around to see if any of the cultists were either nearby, or approaching the prison shed.

Finally, after determining that the coast was clear and she could now take her leave of this awful place, Shirley squeezed through the space and stood up outside the shed.

Once more, pressed up against the wall in the shadows, she looked cautiously around her, on the alert for any nearby motion. Her erstwhile prison was situated at one end of the central driveway between the parked automobiles. From where she stood, she could see past the altar and clear down to the gate at the far end of the yard. The gate was wide open.

She considered her options. She could go in the opposite direction: head for the perimeter fence and try to clamber over it and thus reach safety. That was the most obvious way out of here. She measured the height of the fence with her eyes—five or six feet at most; and it wasn't topped with razor wire either. She could scale it with very little difficulty. Ten minutes tops and she'd be safe in the woods.

But what then? Because what I'm thinking here is obviously what Ted thought too and look where it got him.

While working she'd managed to force all thoughts of Ted to the back of her mind. That had been the only way she'd been able to keep digging; otherwise, she would have given up and waited to be butchered and fed to the pigs also. But now, the memory of his death—just a few hours ago, and after traveling all the way here from Pittsburgh to rescue her—swamped her again and threatened to destroy her resolve.

If I head into the woods, that's surely the first place they'll look once they find I'm gone. They'll comb the woods for me and by morning I'll most likely be back here, tied up this time—she stole a nervous look back at the pig pen—*or worse even . . .*

Two of the hogs noticed her looking their way and stared back at her expectantly, oinking and shoving their bloody snouts between the gaps in the pen's wooden railing.

So, I'd better steal a car and drive away from here. The yard is silent. Hopefully, I'll be gone, with a good head start before the cultists can organize themselves into a posse to hunt me down.

This decided, Shirley made her way past the pig pen and crept into one of the nearby driveways between the cars, one that ran directly by the altar and which she believed would bring her close to Ted's BMW.

Taking Ted's car was clearly out of the question anyway—she didn't have the keys. But, speaking of car keys, she doubted that most of the cultists who'd parked their vehicles here in the impound yard would have bothered removing their keys from the ignition.

At least she hoped they wouldn't have. *I just need to find one car . . .*

With the noise of the hogs slowly diminishing behind her, Shirley made her cautious progress towards the center of the impound yard.

CHAPTER 51

Star was almost done cleaning now. She laughed with amusement when she gazed over at the altar. Cleaned up and with the sacrificial table folded away out of sight, it once more looked like the modern art sculpture celebrating 'the fusion of man and machine' that Buffalo bullshitted folks that it was.

She wiped her right forearm across her forehead and stared down at the yard's front gate. *Well, sure there's no chance of anything going wrong here at 3 a.m. in the morning, but why the hell must Leroy leave the darn gate wide open like that? And tonight of all nights—he knows there's never a guard available once we have a celebration. Guards are human too: once they've danced and gotten drunk and fucked a girl, all they wanna do is sleep.*

Star shrugged. There was really nothing to worry about; what with the mean and nasty men currently present with her in the yard. Just thinking of the men gave Star an immense morale boost. She'd be the first one to admit that she was an *evil* woman, one who'd aligned herself to the ways of darkness, and an evil woman naturally attracted evil men. That was the way of the world, and had always—ever since she'd understood the path of the Wolf and Rabbit—been the way of her own life.

Star had no time for 'nice' folk—she was what she was and she was proud of it. Over the years she'd killed many people; most of whom it could be argued hadn't deserved it. Did she feel any remorse for her actions? Did she give a shit? Hell no, she didn't care one bit—those she'd sacrificed during her own time wearing the identity of the Wolf-Rabbit Deity had simply been means to an end, that end being the worship of the goddess Oryctolupus and the securing of her blessing upon the clan.

As she'd taught April and May when they were young: *Just as the wolf preys on the rabbit, we too prey on those weaker and less powerful than us.*

So, for sure, knowing the violent capabilities of her male companions here tonight, Star figured she had no reason at all to worry.

Still, she sighed and glanced up at the cold sky, at the face of the moon. *So then, why the hell do I still feel uneasy?*

She looked around in case a pair of hostile eyes were studying her, but could see no one, and yet her eerie feeling persisted.

Star didn't like how she felt one bit. Something wasn't right. She resolved to get into the office with the men as quickly as she could.

She moved quickly now, collecting up the cleaning items—bottles of bleach and detergents, brushes and cloths—into a large cleaning cart.

CHAPTER 52

Shirley reached the altar and paused. From here she had a clear view of Ted's BMW and also of the cultists' own parked vehicles.

Before proceeding further however, she decided to make sure the impound gate was still open. So, she crossed the short distance over to the yard's central driveway again and peered down it. Yes, the main gate was still open; but for how much longer that would be the case, she couldn't guess.

Bent low so the cars concealed her from view, she dashed back over to near the altar, gazing up at the sky as she went. The air was cold and the moon was hiding again. Shirley was no expert at reading the sky, but she knew it would soon be morning and she needed to be far gone from here before then.

She was well-concealed where she stood now, hidden between a pickup truck and a rusted old Nissan sedan that must have been in the yard for decades. Front and back of those she was surrounded by high grass that made her practically invisible to her captors. Anyone observing her position would be completely oblivious to her presence here, but she couldn't remain here, could she? It was frustrating to realize that she needed to step out of such an inconspicuous, if only temporary, safe haven and move on.

The altar loomed directly ahead of her. A huge morbid construct, the very sight of which terrified her. She would have preferred to skirt around it, but here was where all the cultists had parked their cars. If she wanted to steal a ride out of here, she had no choice but to approach this evil altar. She looked up at it, but from this rear perspective and her angle of concealment, the sacrificial table was obscured by the curtain of hubcaps through which the clan's priestess had emerged.

The main impound office stood maybe thirty yards off from the left of the altar. About half of the building's windows were lit, including those in the front offices. Which meant someone was still up in there.

Meaning I need to be deathly quiet; quieter than a mouse even.

She scanned the area again with a cautious gaze, and then relaxed slightly. All looked clear, the world seemed quiet and still. Time to move on.

Feeling nervous, she bit her lip.

After taking a deep breath to steady her nerves, Shirley sneaked out of hiding. However, after she had taken a few steps she froze in fright. She had heard movement.

Oh, there's someone over there . . . on the other side of the altar.

Shirley listened and after a while the sound came again. Footsteps. She listened harder. *It sounds like just one person, not a group of them.*

She saw no point in retreating again, and so to conceal herself, she instead stepped up close to the rear of the altar. On doing so however, the altar's metal components shifted slightly as she pressed her body against them. She was surprised by this; she had imagined it as a solid construction. But no, a slight investigating shove made her realize that, while the central portion with the tire steps and the sacrificial table might have been welded firmly together, this more peripheral area of it that she stood beside was precariously balanced and might topple over if she leaned too hard on it.

Ahead of her, around the altar's side, a projecting car bumper appeared to have simply been shoved into place and appeared about to fall out of position again. And on the floor by her feet were several smaller objects—like spark plugs for instance—that seemed to have actually fallen out of the altar.

All this she hastily observed while she considered her present dilemma: *I can either wait here until whoever is still near the altar has left and then I can leave myself . . . or I can move on and try to avoid him or her.*

But waiting was danger. The longer she waited, the greater was the likelihood that someone would find and recapture her.

She decided to move forward and stepped around the side of the altar now to see who was still working there. The yard lights were bright around her and so she hurried. As she dodged the altar's many spiky projections, she realized that all of the animal skins and skeletons that had decorated it had been removed. She also quickly became aware of the smell of cleansing agents—detergent and bleach.

So they've been cleaning up the evidence. As horrific as the realization was, she understood that in this case the cultists' action was the logical one: otherwise the local authorities would long ago have caught on to the fact that very illegal happenings had been going on in here. And from what she'd heard some of the cultists say during her short time in their captivity, the clan's murderous 'sacrifices' extended back almost thirty years—in fact, to well before both April and May were born.

She was on the same side of the altar as her erstwhile cage. She spat at the cage in horror and wonder.

Oops. Shirley had been so deep in thought that she'd almost kicked over a bottle of bleach, one that, along with a set of brushes, stood on a tray left down on the ground. She realized her good luck; had she kicked the bottle over, she would have alerted the person at the front of the altar to her presence here.

That person was just around the corner. In fact, Shirley thought that she heard footsteps approaching right now.

Alarmed, she froze and ducked into what shadow she could find.

She was still hiding herself when Star, dressed in an old dress and a cleaning apron, walked around the edge of the altar.

Star was carrying a tray of cleaning items and she seemed nervous as she swung around the corner, not noticing Shirley until she was right in front of her.

On seeing who it was, Shirley's worries and fright immediately erupted into rage. Before Star had a chance to even exclaim her surprise, Shirley leapt on her and knocked her off her feet.

They both fell to the ground, with Star's cleaning goods scattering everywhere.

Star quickly got over her surprise at Shirley's freedom. The fall had winded her and she was struggling to breathe.

Shirley, who understood exactly what was going to happen if Star managed to get enough air in her lungs to scream for help, quickly grabbed up one of Star's cleaning rags from the grass where it had fallen. Then she jumped on top of Star and straddled her chest, and then forced the bunched up-cloth into Star's mouth. While Star flailed against her, Shirley worked the dirty rag deep and tightly in between her lips, completely muffling her desperate cries.

With no way to call for help, Star's eyes widened in panic. She struggled, flailing like a beached fish. She reached for Shirley's throat and squeezed, choking her.

Shirley had never been this violent before in her life; but then, she had never felt this enraged before either. She didn't regard Star as a human being, but rather as a wild animal—perhaps a dog turned rabid—attacking her. She'd already seen two murders tonight and knew her life was on the line now.

As Star's fingers tightened around her throat, Shirley, who was still sitting on Star's chest, grabbed up a bottle of bleach, twisted it open and poured it into Star's eyes.

The effect was immediate. Star gave out a muffled howl through her gag and her hands instantly let go of Shirley's neck and instead flew up to her own face. While kicking and bucking in pain, she began rubbing fiercely at her eyes. Shirley poured more bleach over Star's hands and face, ensuring that she was rubbing the solution into her eyes, and then she got up and hurried over to the altar.

There, she grabbed the loose length of car bumper that she had earlier noticed amidst the tower of car parts and yanked it as hard as she could. Once the bumper fell free of the pile, she dragged it over towards Star.

With death in her gaze, she knelt down over Star again.

By now Star had blindly started to pull the cleaning rag out of her mouth, her muffled screams becoming marginally louder. At the moment she sounded like a mewling kitten. Shirley didn't intend to let her get any louder.

"Oh no, you don't, bitch!" Shirley whispered to her.

After punching Star in the gut and knocking Star's hands away from her mouth, Shirley stuffed the cleaning rag back down between her lips before reaching over with both hands to give the bumper one last heave, so that now it was poised over Star's body.

Star, of course couldn't see what was about to happen to her.

Shirley positioned the car bumper across Star's throat and then pressed down on it. Star's eyes popped out wildly. She stopped rubbing her eyes and tried to push the bumper away from her neck. But Shirley wasn't about letting go. Instead, she added a lot more weight on the length of metal, leaning forward and bearing down extra hard on it for several minutes until Star stopped struggling and lay still beneath her, her damaged eyes open and glassy.

Panting, Shirley got up. For a few seconds she looked around frantically. And then she hurried over to the car-part altar and picked up two sharp pieces of metal that had become dislodged from it when she'd freed the bumper.

Then she ran towards one of the nearest cars, one of those which she remembered as belonging to a cultist. She pulled open the car door, and checked inside, fingering around the ignition.

"Shit!" she exclaimed on realizing that there was no keys in the ignition.

Leaving the car door open, she ran to the next 'cultist' car. But here also she was doomed to face disappointment. She tugged at the car door, but found it was locked.

"Fuck!" she grunted in a voice as hurt and guttural as the dying moans of a shot hog.

The next car in line was T-Bird's police cruiser. No point in even checking out that one.

She ducked down beside the second car and looked around. The rest of the cars near her weren't newly arrived, most carried the dust of age on them. She glanced over at Ted's BMW. If only . . .

She looked over at the impound offices, and wondered how long it would be before someone would realize that Star was late in returning from her excellent cleaning job. Because from where Shirley stood, the evil altar no longer looked anything like the bloody mess it had earlier in the night when Ted had died on it.

Remembering what had happened to Ted, Shirley again felt both distressed and lost. But then, on looking over at Star's corpse, she also felt a sense of accomplishment. She felt both strong and purposeful.

Shirley reached a decision, and ran up the driveway towards the gate.

CHAPTER 53

In the wide front room of the main impound yard office, Big Jim and T-Bird both sat drinking whiskey.

Sitting here drinking like this had become something of a tradition for them both over the years, as Star was compulsive about getting the Wolf-Rabbit deity's altar spanking clean, and T-Bird always had to wait to drive her home afterwards.

T-Bird's old lady is a little weird in the head for sure, Big Jim thought as he raised his glass of whiskey to his lips. Star never agreed to let the younger—and stronger—clan women handle the cleaning. She'd do it all herself, and then—according to T-Bird—she'd spend the next week or two complaining that her back was killing her.

"What you laughing 'bout?" T-Bird asked on noticing Big Jim's smile.

"Uh, nuthin', " Big Jim replied, knowing how protective of Star the sheriff was. "Just thinkin' it's great how great a cleanin' job on the altar Star keeps doin'. All these years and no one's ever had the slightest inklin' what really goes on in here."

T-Bird nodded. "Yeah. Our goddess Oryctolupus sure does protect her own, don't she?"

"That she does," Big Jim agreed. He stared at his empty glass and then at the whiskey bottle, did a mental calculation, and then said:

"Yup, that's all for me, unless I wanna wrap my ride 'round a tree." Then he leered at T-Bird. "Think I'll go have me some more fun with the gal before I go. You an' Buffalo ain't the only ones got a woman for the night."

T-Bird waved his own glass at Big Jim and laughed. "You'll be lucky to get it up—the amount of Wild Turkey you've drunk."

171

Big Jim laughed. "No worries there. Ain't you heard the saying 'Big Jim's a-comin'!?' I tell ya, Tee, Big Jim's always ready. Except . . . I am pretty tired, right now . . . and just a li'l bit drunk."

They both laughed at that.

T-Bird drained his glass and got up. "Yeah, right. Hey, well, I gotta be off—go find Star and May, if she ain't gone already. I'll leave you two lovebirds alone."

Big Jim patted his belly and chuckled. "Ha ha. Lovebirds, yourself." He began singing in a tipsy, mocking voice: "Star and T-Bird, sittin' in a tree . . ."

T-Bird finishing the rhyme for him: "K.I.L.L.I.N.G."

Big Jim burst into a loud belly laugh.

T-Bird waved at him and left.

CHAPTER 54

Leroy swung the main gate closed and locked it with one of a set of keys.

Then, whistling, he pocketed the keys. Leroy was still smarting a little from Star's earlier hassling of him. But he had to admit that she had a point. It was a damn good point too; they couldn't be too careful where security was concerned.

But still, by leaving the gate unlocked for a while longer than was usual, he'd made his own point: he wasn't here to be pushed around by Star.

Leroy took orders from her husband T-Bird, and even there grudgingly. Leroy didn't like any members of T-Bird's family very much: the husband was too egotistic; the wife a borderline-crazy bitch. And the daughters? Well, as far as Leroy was concerned. The less said about those two the better . . .

Leroy felt intense pity for whoever got hitched to either of T-Bird's kids; except if possibly the guy was as crazy as T-Bird was.

But even if Leroy disliked his compatriots in murder and criminal endeavors, (as there was no denying that the illegal chop shop the impound yard fronted for made them all a regular and tidy sum of money), he was a full devotee of the Wolf-Rabbit deity Oryctolupus and sworn to protect her clan with his life's blood.

"And so, I'll lock the gate like a good boy and keep watch, like the manic-excitable lady says . . ."

While thus reflecting, Leroy had been staring out through the gate, his gaze fixed on the dirt road that wound out to the highway and from there connected with the normal world; a world where dark pursuits such as had happened here scant hours ago were considered evil and despicable.

But now, thinking he heard movement nearby, Leroy looked around. And then, not noticing anything out of the ordinary, he figured he was imagining things.

He removed a cigarette lighter from the pocket he'd dropped the keys into and set fire to the plastic sack in his hand, holding it at arm's length so it didn't burn him.

Leroy grinned, entranced by the quickly roaring flames and the pungent black smoke that suddenly enveloped him.

But then, as the flames and smoke died down and Leroy dropped the sack's burning remains on the ground, he suddenly saw something completely unexpected—the face of their female captive looming there at close range. And the girl looked manic and determined.

Leroy was taken completely off guard. He reeled back in shock, staggering, desperate not to loose his balance. *What was her name again?* he wondered as she came quickly towards him. *Yeah, Shirley.* Shirley looked really pissed off; as indeed Leroy figured she would be after all that they'd done to her, particularly Big Jim.

"Whoa! How da hell'd you git free?" he asked.

But the young woman never answered the question. She was already leaping at him and slashing at his throat with her makeshift weapons.

Still too surprised to yell for help, Leroy gasped in surprise as one of Shirley's weapons caught him in the neck.

CHAPTER 55

Unaware that things had begun falling to pieces around his ears, T-Bird wandered through the yard, towards the altar.

Okay, so maybe I shouldn't'a drunk so much whiskey. I ain't too firm on my legs at the moment. Night air's helpin' sober me up a trifle anyways . . .

T-Bird reached the altar.

"Hey, Star! You ready to go?"

He was surprised that silence was the only reply he got. Star should be out here for sure; dog-tired on her feet as usual and ready to fall asleep in the car on their drive home; after which he'd have to practically carry her into the house and put her to bed.

"Hey, Star, where are ya!?" he called. She was clearly still out here. Her cleaning cart was laden up and ready to be returned to the office.

When his second shouted inquiry brought no response either, T-Bird set off walking around the left side of the altar, and then pulled up short.

He blinked and then blinked again. Star was lying there on the ground motionless.

"What the . . . ?" Seeing the car bumper lying across her neck, T-Bird at first thought his wife had suffered an accident while cleaning.

But, while subsequently running across to her, he caught sight of the rag stuffed in her mouth; and the smell of spilled bleach hit him too.

Once by Star's side, T-Bird crouched and lifted the car bumper off of her throat and flung it aside. He felt her throat for her pulse, but already knew that it was useless. Her eyes looked bloody and wounded, but above the damage they'd suffered, they also looked empty and lifeless. Still he took her pulse. Then he remained kneeling next to her, shaking her shoulders.

"Star? Star, baby?" he moaned in deep emotional turmoil.

After a while of doing this, T-Bird got to his feet. Shattered and confused, uncertain what do next, he stumbled about, both looking and feeling disorientated.

For the moment, this made no sense. Who the hell had killed Star?

"Jim! Jim!" he shouted back towards the impound office to get Big Jim's attention.

CHAPTER 56

Shirley stabbed Leroy madly, taking out her frustration on him. At first, he fought back against her, and his desperate strength made her wonder if she'd not made a mistake in attacking him head-on.

But she was much more desperate than he was.

Leroy groaned in pain and spilled blood over her hands and body. She'd intentionally stabbed him in the throat first. She couldn't take any chance on his alerting the others. He pummeled at her with his fists, catching her in the face a couple of times, but she was relentless, high on adrenalin.

Shirley grunted she worked Leroy over with her sharp metal weapons; emitting the low guttural sounds to the same rhythm as that of her stabbing hands.

She soon realized she was winning their conflict of violent wills. Leroy was much stronger than she, but with his throat punctured and his blood spraying and pumping out of him from the many wounds she kept afflicting on him he had no choice but to weaken.

Shirley's face was spattered with the spray of Leroy's blood and she had to blink to see clearly, but she battled on regardless, stabbing and slashing repeatedly, until Leroy finally slumped against her, then fell to the floor, where he groaned, and lay still and dead.

CHAPTER 57

As T-Bird rushed up towards the hut where Shirley had been imprisoned, Big Jim came hurtling out of the impound office.

"Tee? What d'ya want? Where you at?" he yelled back across the yard as he stood on the office's front porch. *Oh, dammit, what the hell is wrong now.*

Receiving no reply to his shouted inquiry, Big Jim set off running towards the altar. Something definitely was wrong, that was certain. T-Bird's yell had had something mournful in it. And the fact that Big Jim couldn't see either T-Bird or Star standing over by the altar could mean just about anything.

Big Jim was soon forced to admit he'd drunk too much. By the time he'd reached the altar, he was completely out of breath and panting. Sweat was running in rivulets off of his bald head. Still, realizing that something was definitely amiss, and feeling a slight surge of panic beginning in his cold and jaded mind, he stumbled around the side of the altar and found Star lying on the ground there.

Big Jim immediately put two and two together: "Oh, shit! Tee!"

Staring at Star's corpse, Big Jim felt as if tears were going to come rushing to his eyes (he'd loved his sister almost as much as her husband did) but then he heard the sound of running footsteps.

He looked up. T-Bird was rushing towards him from the direction of the pig pen at the north end of the impound yard. Big Jim read hurt and loss in T-Bird's face, but that pain also seemed mingled with a huge dose of worry.

"I just checked the hut. Damn girl's gone!" T-Bird said.

Gone? That put a dangerous spin on things. Big Jim understood why T-Bird looked worried as hell. If the girl had escaped, mourning Star's death could wait. Callous as it might seem, they both had bigger things to worry about.

Big Jim suddenly had a horrifying vision of everything—this whole world of religious ecstasy and financial profit that they'd constructed—coming crashing down around them like a brick house hit by tank fire.

"The bitch is gone?" he asked T-Bird in confusion, his fat face wobbling like jelly.

CHAPTER 58

But no, Shirley Wade hadn't yet 'gone,' though she was desperate to do so.

Down by the impound entrance, Shirley was hastily ransacking Leroy's pockets for the keys to the gate.

"Dammit," she spat on discovering that his left pants pocket was empty. His left pocket was however the easy one to search. Leroy had fallen on his right side, and that pants pocket was thus underneath him.

Shirley turned him over. Both she and he were covered with his blood and so it was a messy operation, but it had to be done.

Leroy had fallen to the floor facing away from her, so she couldn't see his face, but now as she rolled him first onto his back and then towards her so that he was lying on his left side, she did see the expression on his face: Leroy had lots of blood on his lips and a look of disbelief in his staring eyes.

Shirley shook her head and spat in his face. "You got just what you deserved, asshole."

She'd gotten him turned over now, and so quickly dug her hand into the pants pocket.

Yes, she thought with a surge of delight and satisfaction as her fingers touched a bunch of cold metal objects in his pocket. She pulled out the keys victoriously. And then, realizing that she was wasting time gloating over her victory, she scrambled up from beside Leroy's prone body and ran over to the impound gate.

The gate was huge and seemed designed to resist her exit. Shirley had a moment or two of panic at first when the first three keys she slotted into the lock didn't fit. Because now, in the predawn silence, she could hear voices, two male voices speaking loudly at the center of the impound yard.

And she recognized who the speakers were—the sheriff and that slob Big Jim.

Panicking now, she slotted another key into the lock. This one turned out to be the right one. Two sharp twists to the left and the lock clicked open.

Gasping in relief, Shirley pushed the gate wide open.

CHAPTER 59

T-Bird pushed Big Jim towards his police cruiser. "Get in the car!"

Big Jim immediately set his large bulk in motion. He didn't need to be told twice. There was absolutely no time to waste if they were to catch the fugitive young woman and avert disaster.

He and T-Bird both flung open the doors of the police car and threw themselves into its front seats. T-Bird stuck the key into the ignition, started the car up, and then they roared off down the driveway. Big Jim held on tight to the edge of his seat as T-Bird swung the cruiser around the hood of the first car in line and sped towards the gate; this promised to be quite a bumpy ride.

Then, as they reached the gate, the cruiser's headlights picked out something on the ground. It seemed both human and bloody.

T-Bird hesitated for a moment and then pulled the cruiser up to a shuddering halt close to the bloody body on the concrete flooring.

Then, with T-Bird leaning over from the driver's side to see more clearly, both men craned their necks out of the passenger side window and peered down at the body on the ground outside.

"Shit, that's Leroy!" Big Jim instantly yelped. "She killed Leroy too?"

T-Bird moved away from the window and settled back over in the driver's seat. "That bitch," he growled, his eyes cold as ice and his voice as deadly as an arctic winter, gesturing out through the open gate at the road and surrounding forest. "She could be anywhere in the woods by now."

Big Jim nodded fiercely over at the sheriff. "We gotta hunt her down and put her out of her misery like the sick bitch she is."

T-Bird put his foot down on the accelerator and the cruiser eased off through the gate. T-Bird drove slowly now. They didn't want to speed past their target and thus miss apprehending her.

Big Jim reached between the seats into the back and pulled out a large floodlight, which he laid on his knees. He was still sweating, had large patches of wetness in his armpits.

T-Bird took his eyes off the road for a moment and glanced over at Big Jim. He nodded when he saw the hunting light. "Yeah, Jim. She can't have got far, and the woods are thin here. Swing that lamp onto the trees and we'll drive by slow. Afterwards, I'll park up over on the other side of the woods, and then we'll work our way back in, on foot."

"Good idea," Big Jim agreed, hocking a large gob of phlegm out of the window. "Any luck, she'll run right into my arms." The thrill of the hunt was on him now and he was beginning to lose his worries that anything could go wrong with their chase.

"And then I'll rip her fucking arms off," T-Bird said savagely. "Hell, after what the murderin' bitch just did to my darlin' Star, I'll rip her fuckin' legs off as well."

Feeling exactly the same, Big Jim switched on the lamp and shone it into trees, which now began looking like ghosts.

CHAPTER 60

Her face an image of hatred, Shirley lay hidden in the dark undergrowth just beyond the impound gate, watching the approaching police cruiser intently.

She gripped her makeshift weapons in white knuckles and waited. This was make-or-break time. The knowledge of what would happen to her if she was recaptured by the corrupt sheriff and the gas-station owner spurred her on. She didn't dare dwell on what they'd do to her for killing both Star and Leroy—a vision of handfuls of her own shredded flesh being pulled out of a plastic sack and thrown over the wooden railing of the pig pen while the swine fought over it and oinked their delight hung before her eyes and threatened to terrify her into leaping up and fleeing into the woods.

But Shirley had already realized that fleeing would be counterproductive here. If she ran she would simply draw attention to herself, and even if both men were too tired or drunk (or in Big Jim's case—too overweight) to run fast after her the sheriff at least, had a gun.

So, she remained motionless where she was as the police cruiser's headlight swept over the grass outside the gate. And afterwards, when the floodlight clicked on in the vehicle and she watched Big Jim play its beam across the grass and trees, she merely slithered backward on her belly like a snake, further back into the brush, ensuring she wouldn't be noticed by the two men in the car.

The floodlight played right over her head when the cruiser paused for a few seconds after Big Jim had snapped it on, when he aimed the light backwards in case he'd missed her.

When that happened, she kept as still as she could; trying not to even breathe. Had the light fallen directly on her then, it would have revealed that rather than being a mask of panic and terror, her white face was sullen and determined, and her blue eyes burned with a bloodlust that would have in turn scared those hunting her.

Still holding her breath, Shirley watched the police cruiser drive off slowly away from the yard, with Big Jim shining the beam first through the car window on his side and then through the other.

When the men in the car were a good distance down the road with no chance of noticing her anymore, she got up and tentatively looked around. She realized that she'd successfully thrown her pursuers off her scent.

"Okay, time to go." She opened her left hand and stared down at its contents.

Along with one of the metal spikes that she'd so far been using as a weapon, she was holding the bunch of keys that she had taken from Leroy.

The keys were strung on a large car key ring. Shirley studied them for a while, then she sifted through them and picked out the actual car key itself.

Now she smiled. Her eyes cautiously tracked back up the impound's main driveway. The aisle was empty. Everywhere seemed peaceful.

Thanks, Leroy, you asshole, she thought. *Your ride is going to be my ride out of here.*

That settled, Shirley reentered the impound yard and ran back towards its center, keeping to the shadows just in case someone was lurking in wait.

CHAPTER 61

After a while of driving, T-Bird pulled the police cruiser over to the side of the road and parked just outside the tree line.

He and Big Jim both got out, carrying guns and flashlights. Both of them now also had walkie-talkies clipped to their belts. As they stepped beneath the trees, T-Bird checked the fluorescent hands of his wristwatch.

"Dammit, soon be daylight," he announced to his partner-in-crime.

Big Jim considered the information: "Sure you don't wanna call out the boys?" he asked. "Get some reinforcements?"

T-Bird shook his head vehemently. "Nah, gettin' more people out here'll take too long. An' besides, it's one skinny little bitch with no strength. We can handle this. Even if she manages to evade *us*, she won't escape May's animal traps. She's got them scattered all over this area. Just a matter of time till she steps in one of 'em."

Big Jim smiled. He liked the sound of that all right: blood and pain. "Hah, yeah. Guess we'll soon hear her scream all right. One way or another."

T-Bird nodded and pushed some tree branches out of the way. Then, not wanting to switch on his flashlight just yet, he squinted in through the woods as deep as he could, trying to find the runaway girl.

"Damn right," he agreed. "I'll rip her apart with my bare hands for what she's done to my Star."

Big Jim felt sad again. "Sorry for your loss, man. Sis didn't deserve that." He flicked on his own torchlight but dimmed the glare. "So, how we gonna do this?" he enquired. "How do we search?"

T-Bird gestured to his right, across the squad car, towards the trees on the opposite side of the dirt road. "You spread out over there," he instructed Big Jim. "Try not to alert her to our presence. Keep your flashlight off or low till you need it."

"Gotcha. Hey, you want her dead or alive?"

"Alive, preferably. But kill her if you got to."

That settled, the two men spilt up, with T-Bird stepping into the woods directly ahead of him and Big Jim hurrying across the road and entering the woods on that side.

CHAPTER 62

Shirley located Leroy's car by a simple process of elimination. His car had to be one of those that had been parked alongside the sheriff's cruiser. She ran over there and from an angle aimed the car key at the foremost four vehicles, and then pressed the button on the key fob.

The second car she had earlier tested—the one that she'd abandoned because it was locked—immediately came alive. Its loud bleep as it unlocked made her freeze for a moment, hoping no one had heard the car.

Once certain that no one had heard the vehicle's noise, Shirley swung open the car door and sat down in the driver's seat.

Even though a quick look around showed her that no one was nearby, she still felt very nervous and fiddled about to slot the key into the ignition. Then she thought she heard a sudden noise nearby and dropped the key altogether.

Shit! she thought in frustration and bent towards the foot well to retrieve the key.

She found it quickly enough, but when she straightened up again and once more tried to slot the key into the ignition, she caught a flash of motion over on her left side.

"Going somewhere?" asked a familiar voice.

Shirley attempted to turn that way to see the speaker, but May had already looped a leather thong down over her head.

Alert to the danger, Shirley got her left hand up just before the loop settled around her throat. In this position May couldn't successfully throttle her, but still she was being pulled out through the car window.

"Nah, I don't think you're going anywhere," May added.

As May attempted to tighten the garrote around her neck, Shirley let go of the car keys and instead grabbed up one of the blood-smeared and weaponized car parts which now lay in her lap, kept there in case of any further danger she encountered while driving.

A contest of strength and wills now ensued, with May doing her best to throttle Shirley, while Shirley likewise did her best to slot her weapon up beneath the leather garrote. Finally she got it done, but May had now braced her knee against the car door and was pulling the garrote tighter with both fists. May's face strained with the effort.

With veins bulging in her neck as the leather tightened around Shirley's throat, she now discovered that she was in additional danger of her makeshift blade piercing her neck.

Grimacing, May pulled the garrote tighter still, while Shirley pushed the metal weapon away from her, holding off both the biting steel and the strangling leather.

And then suddenly, the leather thong gave—it had been cut in half by the metal.

Shirley felt instant relief.

Caught off balance when her garrote snapped, May was propelled away from the car and hit the ground hard. But she leapt up at once, flung away the snapped garrote and pulled another one from her pants' pocket.

She spat at Shirley. "You're dead meat, bitch. You killed my mammy and now I'm gonna kill you too!"

The murderous look in May's eyes chilled Shirley to the bone. She remembered that May was a trapper by profession, and as such was well versed in methods of killing. She also realized that, panicked and winded like she was now, she'd never get the car started before May attacked her again, so she opened the car door and ran for it.

With a plan forming in her mind, she headed for the altar of car parts.

As her feet pounded across the intervening distance, she heard May's footsteps following. She didn't need to look back to know that May was gaining on her.

She leapt over Star's corpse and ducked behind the altar. Then she quickly located that particular side area in the metal pile that had earlier felt less stable that the rest of it.

As May reached the altar and cautiously slowed to a walking pace, Shirley leaned on and shoved the weak-seeming portion of it with all of her might. After a few seconds of exertion, that precariously stacked portion of the alter toppled towards May.

Shirley winced at the loudness of its crash. Her plan of leaving here silently wasn't working out at all.

But her battle strategy appeared to have worked. She heard a terrified scream from May, and then there was silence again.

Relieved, Shirley stepped warily out from behind the altar. Surrounded by scattered hubcaps, May was lying on the ground. She didn't look dead, but she seemed to have been knocked unconscious.

Shirley walked quickly towards her, intending to finish her off, but then she gasped in alarm. May, who was unharmed and had just been playing possum, quickly got up from the ground. An evil grin on her face, she grabbed Shirley's arm and attempted to loop a garrote over her head again.

Shirley escaped being caught in the lethal leather loop and punched May, who gasped with pain and dropped her garrote, but who in turn tripped Shirley up. Shirley held on tight to her while falling, however, and so they both dropped to the ground together.

The young women wrestled for dominance, rolling left and right on the ground amongst the scattered car parts.

Then, as they rolled up against the mechanical rubble that Shirley had just toppled over, Shirley noticed a large piece of spiky metal within reaching distance.

She quickly grabbed it and bashed May in the forehead with it. "Die, bitch!"

May had been getting to her feet when Shirley caught her with the chunk of metal. She staggered back, but recovered quickly. With blood streaming down her face, she stood there glaring fiercely at Shirley. Swaying, but unfazed.

Then with a loud scream, she launched herself at Shirley. Shirley waited patiently for May to arrive, and then, with a loud grunt of her own, she bashed her in the head again.

"That's for Ted!" she explained fiercely as the spiked metal object made contact with May's head, much harder this time.

May managed to keep her feet again, but just barely. Gripping Shirley's shoulders to steady herself, and with blood now pouring from a deep wound over her ear and tinting her purple hair red, she gaped up at Shirley in surprise, a dazed expression on her face.

Shirley raised the metal weight high again and dealt May one more blow. Remembering exactly how much the purple-haired girl had gloated over Ted's impending death, she put all of her strength into this one.

'Crack!' May's head sounded like it had just exploded. She collapsed to the floor like dead weight and lay there motionless with her eyes shut, with her body twisted, and with blood flooding out of the fatal crack Shirley had just made in her skull.

Satisfied that she'd successfully dispatched May to Hell, Shirley turned and sprinted for Leroy's car.

She climbed inside the car, and after locating the keys from where they'd fallen when May had been throttling her, she started up the vehicle and eased it out of parking.

Then she turned it towards the entrance of the impound yard and drove away.

CHAPTER 63

Big Jim stepped cautiously through the edge of the woods in the early morning darkness. He stopped and shuddered when his flashlight picked out the details of the open maw and metal teeth of a bear trap he'd been heading for.

Big Jim scowled. "One more step and there went my ankle. Good thing I ain't a deer, right? May's got these damned traps set up all over the place. I need to have a word with her pa 'bout this. But, nah, we ain't 'sposed to be this far out anyway."

He stepped away from the trap and moved onward, walking a bit deeper into the forest now. He figured it was dumb to expect the girl to remain so close to the road anyway.

Big Jim thought back on how sweet the city girl had been; cute blonde hair and a nice body too, with juicy breasts. Young and pretty she was—exactly how he liked them. As he remembered all the perverted things he'd made her do, he decided that if he found her before T-Bird did, he'd do his best not to kill her.

He grinned at the thought. "Nah, best to keep her alive a li'l while yet. I still got a few Big Jim discounts I wanna give to her."

He paused for a moment, scratched his bald head and shone his dimmed flashlight beam into the upper branches of the trees directly ahead.

"No sign of the bitch here on this side of the road tho . . . Wonder how T-Bird's makin' out with his side of the search?"

***

Across the road, T-Bird had just stopped walking beneath the trees and was standing as still and as quiet as he could manage, listening.

Then, not sure of exactly what he was hearing, or if he was hearing anything at all other than the usual sound of woodland critters, he detached the walkie-talkie from his belt and spoke into it, keeping his voice low in case their quarry was nearby:

"Hey, Jim. You hear somethin'?"

A moment later, Big Jim's voice came through: "Where?"

"Direction of the yard."

"Nope . . . nuthin'," Big Jim replied. "Like what kinda sound?"

"Dunno," T-Bird replied and then tried to explain better: "Like a crashing kinda sound? Sounded funny-like . . . like—"

Then T-Bird fell silent because he'd just heard another sound, this time coming from the road behind him. He spun around and looked towards the dirt road, and through the trees saw the car coming from the direction of the impound yard. The car had its headlights turned off, but could be identified as one because of the moonlight glinting off its body and windows.

An instant surge of alarm ran through T-Bird. "Hey, Jim," he told the walkie-talkie, "somebody just drove out of the yard!"

"What? Yeah, I can hear the car engine out on the road. Hey, Tee, you sure it wasn't just May leavin'?"

"Hell no, it cain't be! There's no way May's gonna drive away with her mother lying dead back there!"

"Yeah, you're right. Shit, Tee! Has to be the girl tryin' to git away agin."

"Get back to the car!"

After giving this instruction to Big Jim, T-Bird turned and ran off through the woods himself, out towards the road where he'd parked the police cruiser.

We cain't let her get away! he thought desperately as he raced through a stretch of knee-high grass. *She's gonna ruin everything for us!*

T-Bird was however so alarmed that he wasn't watching where he was going. And a short while later he ran straight into a bear trap that Big Jim earlier noticed and avoided.

T-Bird had a moment of shock and a clear understanding of his mistaken route when he stepped onto a metal plate instead of grass and the trap was sprung. And then the next moment, he screamed out in pain and fell like a chainsawed tree. His walkie-talkie went flying as he hit the ground, and so he even though he yelled for help, there was no chance of his in-law hearing him.

"Ow! Shit! Jim!" T-Bird howled, realizing that they were now staring disaster in the face.

**

In the woods on the other side of the road, Big Jim now saw the car speeding past.

Nah. That ain't May at the wheel! The girl's gettin' away!

Panicking, Big Jim rushed through the trees and made exactly the same mistake as T-Bird had.

He ran around a large tree and then stepped into a snare. Before he even realized what had gone wrong, the snare's rope had looped around his ankle and yanked him high up into the air.

Big Jim suddenly found himself dangling upside down, with just his shoulders and head resting on the ground.

On realizing he had no way to free himself without help, he let out a scream of rage and frustration.

CHAPTER 64

Shirley drove on, hunched down over the wheel. Her initial panic as she sped past the parked police cruiser turned to elation when she discovered to her surprise that there was no pursuit.

After about ten minutes of driving unpursued, she relaxed a little and flicked on the headlights. Now, as the sky began to lighten with daylight, the speeding car seemed to fly over the countryside roads.

However, even though she drove fast and furious, she drove with caution, keeping one eye on the rearview mirror. She wondered what had happened to Big Jim and the sheriff.

I made it, she realized, as she turned onto the interstate and headed north for Pennsylvania, with relief pouring over her like cleansing water. *I made it out alive!*

She didn't feel happy though. Remembering what had happened to Ted, Shirley wondered if she'd ever feel happy again.

EPILOGUE

Two months had passed since Shirley's ordeal at the hands of the Wolf-Rabbit Clan cultists. Today was a beautiful day in the city of Pittsburgh, PA, with lovely sunshine warming the urban landscape.

However, in one office on Carson Street in the south side of Pittsburgh, things were decidedly cooler.

Shirley Wade sat in the office of the Special Agent in Charge, oblivious to the sun streaking in through its large windows.

In contrast to the two days of her regrettable ordeal at the hands of the worshippers of Oryctolupus, Shirley looked clean and tidy now. She was once again dressed smartly, with her hair freshly styled and her nails neatly manicured.

The only things wrong with this picture of an attractive young woman sitting in a pleasant office environment were the blank way she gazed out of the window and the new bottle of antidepressant medication that she kept rolling over and over in her fingers as if scared that it might be stolen from her.

Shirley looked up when the door opened. It was SAC Donaldson coming to once more interview her. The investigator was a tall man with calm probing eyes.

Shirley flinched as he drew near to her, even though he stopped six feet away and pulled up a chair to sit on. He was very aware of what had happened to her. Nowadays she was scared to let people close to her—men in particular, but also women who reminded her of T-Bird's wife and daughters.

Donaldson smiled reassuringly at her. She hardly noticed; she'd returned to staring out of the window. Then, possibly to subconsciously increase the distance between them, she got up and walked over to the window and stood there looking outside of his office.

The sky, where she could see it through the skyscrapers, looked so peaceful. It made her wish she was a bird and could take flight and shed this world's burdens. Everything just felt so tight inside of her.

"How's your treatment going, Shirley?" Agent Donaldson asked quietly.

She shrugged. "Fine, I guess," she replied, not looking back at him. She really wasn't sure if the therapy was doing her any good. The medication she'd been prescribed seemed to stabilize her however, which she figured was a good thing.

He got up also and looked out of the window with her, though remaining a respectful distance away. "It will take you some time to get over it."

"Get over it?" Shirley asked/replied in a brittle voice that sounded like it would snap at any minute. "I don't think it's a thing you ever get over. The things I've seen . . . and done . . . what I've been subjected to . . ."

Agent Donaldson smiled gently, his eyes sympathetic. "Maybe, maybe not. But in my professional experience, given time, even the worst traumas can fade. Maybe you won't forget what happened, but you'll be able to put the past behind you and move on."

They stood there in silence, staring out at the sunny day beyond the window.

"Now I know it's not much of a consolation for what happened to you," the man said kindly, "but at least we have arrested the Sheriff and his cronies. So, you know you're safe now, at least."

Shirley nodded in a distracted way. "You're telling me the nightmare is over, huh?"

He nodded affirmation. "Well, yes."

Shirley laughed sardonically, her voice soft and bitter. Oh yes, the agent meant well with his seemingly 'good' news, but he just didn't understand.

So, she turned to stare at him and the blankness in her gaze filled him with a chill despite the day's warmth. "Not for me, Agent," she explained in a flat voice. "For me, the nightmares continue. Every night. And in the day I get flashbacks. And worse: I have hallucinations . . . deep depression . . . anxiety. And I have physical symptoms too—sickness and pain. They say it's Post Traumatic Stress Disorder.

She stared coldly, directly into his eyes, and he flinched. He felt as if he were wilting, being frostbitten by her frigid gaze.

"So actually, no, sir," Shirley finished softly. "For me the nightmare is never over."

The agent shook his head sadly. "I'm sorry, Shirley. So very sorry."

They stood there staring out of the office window, both feeling as if all the warmth had been sucked out of the day.

***

Back home from Agent Donaldson's meeting, Shirley closed her front door and picked up her mail from the floor. Then she flung her purse and jacket down on a sofa and afterwards walked into the kitchenette of her apartment to make herself a cup of coffee.

In the kitchenette, she switched on the kettle, opened a jar of instant coffee and added a spoonful to a cup.

While waiting for the kettle to boil, she began checking out her stack of mail, opening up the top envelope. She read through the letter the envelope contained, an advertisement for DirectTV, but was distracted by the gentle breeze blowing in from the window over the sink. The wind was making the curtain dance just out of the corner of her eye.

Thankfully the kettle boiled then, so that she didn't have to worry about whether or not she wanted to close the window. Shirley poured the water into the cup, added cream and sugar and then carried the mug of steaming coffee into the living area.

She switched on the TV and then leaned back on her couch with the pile of correspondence beside her, which she examined while sipping her coffee.

Then suddenly she set down her coffee on the coffee table.

Shirley frowned at the large envelope she'd just reached, this one addressed to her in red marker pen. She didn't know why, but she felt as if something was wrong about the envelope and its contents. Feeling confused, she leaned forward and scrutinized the handwriting; but it didn't seem to be that of anyone she knew.

Finally, at a loss for what to do, she ripped open the envelope and discovered that it contained just a single glossy photograph. She drew the photograph out, stared at it, and gasped.

What she held in her fingers was a photograph of the female Wolf-Rabbit Deity.

The sight was so unexpected after all this while that Shirley began to hyperventilate. Her hands felt nerveless. They parted and the photograph fluttered to the floor.

Then—"April Fool!"—a voice shrieked behind her, startling her to her bones.

Shirley knew the voice. But here? In her apartment of all places? And now, just after Agent Donaldson had told her that she was safe?

With her eyes widening in fear, Shirley slowly turned around.

The Clan's priestess stood there behind Shirley. She was dressed in her full Wolf-Rabbit Deity costume, but in this case with its mask raised to reveal her face.

Shirley gasped on seeing that the priestess was May's sister April. April Bird, the conservative Ringo County records keeper.

As Shirley now understood that it had been April and not May who had killed Ted that fateful night, April lowered the mask and smirked at her.

"You *may* have killed May, but you didn't get *me*, bitch!" April said gleefully, her voice ringing with sadistic joy.

She hurried around the couch towards Shirley, and Shirley now saw that April was holding her brutal spiked club made from an aluminum baseball bat.

Shirley tried to summon the energy to defend herself, but her surprise was so complete as to render her defenseless. And besides,

April was already swinging the baseball bat at her head and she had no way to escape its deadly trajectory.

And once the spiked club made its first violent contact with her head and ripped the skin off of her face, Shirley understood that she was going to die here and now, and that when she was dead the Wolf-Rabbit goddess Oryctolupus would revive her clan and would once more hold her unholy sacrifices in the dead of night, deep in the West Virginian woods, before a crowd of her rapturous devotees.

"And with every new sacrifice," April solemnly intoned, "with every drop of blood that is spilled, the clan grows in strength."

And by the time Shirley understood this terrifying truth, April was already swinging the bat again to finish her off . . .

The End.

ABOUT THE AUTHOR

Gary Lee Vincent was born in Clarksburg, West Virginia and is an accomplished author, musician, actor, producer, director and entrepreneur. In 2010, his horror novel *Darkened Hills* was selected as 2010 Book of the Year winner by *Foreword Reviews Magazine* and became the pilot novel for *DARKENED - THE WEST VIRGINIA VAMPIRE SERIES*, that encompasses the novels *Darkened Hills, Darkened Hollows, Darkened Waters, Darkened Souls, Darkened Minds* and *Darkened Destinies*. He has also authored the bizarro thriller *Passageway,* a tribute to H.P. Lovecraft, and *When the Bedposts Shake*, an erotic horror.

Gary co-authored the novel *Belly Timber* with John Russo, Solon Tsangaras, Dustin Kay and Ken Wallace, and co-authored the novel *Attack of the Melonheads* with Bob Gray and Solon Tsangaras.

As an actor, Gary has appeared in over seventy feature films and multiple television series, including *House of Cards, Mindhunter, The Walking Dead*, and *Stranger Things*.

As a director, Gary got his directorial debut with *A Promise to Astrid*. He has also directed the films *Desk Clerk, Dispatched*, the 2020 remake of John Russo's iconic horror film *Midnight, Godsend*, and *Strange Friends*.

WHEN THE
BEDPOSTS
SHAKE

AN EROTIC TERROR

GARY LEE VINCENT

WHEN THE BEDPOSTS SHAKE
(RING OF THE SUCCUBUS)

Jack Crannson was having a midlife crisis. A successful architect, Jack was more interest in running his business than saving his marriage. With his workaholic wife fueling his own disinterest, he decides to move closer to his work by purchasing an older house in the Maple Lake section of Bridgeport, West Virginia.

The house purchase seemed like a logical enough choice for Jack, despite Samantha, his estranged wife's, protest. The only illogical thing was the condition that came with the house from Mr. Bannering, the home's previous owner. . .

Mr. Bannering warned that Jack mustn't use the north bedroom, and under no circumstances, sleep in the bed. It was locked and needed to stay that way.

What Mr. Bannering failed to disclose was that trapped within that room was a demonic force, a she-devil succubus named Cali that was looking for some way to escape her prison and enter the earthly realm in the flesh to prey on male victims by feeding on their sexual energy. With the house having a new owner, she may just get her wish.

Warning: this novel contains language intended for an adult audience.

2010 Book of the Year WINNER
ForeWord Reviews Magazine

DARKENED
HILLS

GARY LEE VINCENT

DARKENED HILLS
DARKENED – THE WEST VIRGINIA VAMPIRE SERIES
Book I by Gary Lee Vincent

"2010 Book of the Year WINNER"
- Foreword Reviews Magazine

A tale of gripping psychological horror!

When evil descends on a small West Virginia town, who will survive?

Jonathan did not start out his life to become a rambler, it just worked out that way. William was a troubled youth with something to hide. Both were from Melas, a small town tucked away in the West Virginia hills... a town where disappearances are happening more and more frequently.

After the suicide of a wanted serial killer, the townsfolk thought the nightmare was over. But when a centuries-old vampire is discovered they find out the hard way it's just getting started.

Dark secrets can only stay hidden for so long and when the devil comes to collect, there will be hell to pay. Can Jonathan and William find a way to stop the vampire before it's too late? Find out in Darkened Hills!

Darkened Hills is a gothic vampire novel written in the spirit of Dracula with much more sinister characters and eroticism then the old Victorian classic.

For series information, visit **www.DarkenedHills.com.**

Available on DVD and Blu-Ray

Order direct at
www.MIDNIGHT.rocks